The Eight-Hour Clock

and Other Tales

Best wishes

The Eight-Hour Clock
and Other Tales

G. S. McNern

Precious Chick
Publishing

The Eight Hour Clock and Other Tales
ISBN 0-9546264-0-0

Published by
Precious Chick Publishing
P.O. Box 56, Wellingborough, NN8 1SF
www.preciouschickpublishing.com

Typesetting and artwork by:
TJGraphics Ltd. Tel: 07710 423689 Email: tjgraphics_2000@yahoo.com

Printed and bound in Great Britain by:
Impress Print Ltd. Tel: 01536 402393 Email: sales@impress-print.co.uk

For Sylvia Kingsland,
much missed friend
and fellow dealer, who gave me
tremendous encouragement.

Many thanks:

To David Buchan and to Niki Harford for great chats at fairs which sowed some seeds for my imagination to work on.

And to John Gammons, whom I also met at a fair and inflicted on him almost everything I've ever written, who not only still speaks to me but has been a most helpful guide in the publishing maze.

Special thanks to David Smith for - oh, lots of things.

Thanks, too, to my mum, Sophia, without whom none of this would have been possible, and to my daughter, Samantha, (my one precious chick!) for her faith in me and her support, and thanks to her husband, Jamie, for his.

I'd better also thank Judy who first called my daughter that many years ago and inadvertently gave me such a useful future publishing title.

The Eight-Hour Clock
and Other Tales

Contents

The Eight-Hour Clock

There is no such thing as an eight-hour clock. It would be like a car with a thimble-sized petrol tank. Imagine a clock you had to get up and wind every eight hours. No-one would want one. But lots of people wanted the one that became known in the trade as the eight-hour clock.

"Oi! You, Blondie!"

The man's sneering tone set my teeth on edge. Especially when I realised he was addressing me.

Without waiting for a response, he called the colour and number of my vehicle loudly across the cattle shed. A cattle shed, I have to say, still richly redolent of the livestock sales held here a few days before today's Antiques and Collectors Fair in spite of it having been hosed down.

We in the antiques trade often share premises with those in the meat trade. That sort of thing helps you keep the business in perspective.

"Yours innit, Blondie? Well, get it shifted! I can't get me sideboard off me wagon!"

I had arrived on-site at 7am when the traditional early trading between dealers had made the car-park buzz. Some dealers made their best sales and their best purchases then, buying and selling from the backs of their vehicles before being allowed entry to the buildings at 8am.

I sell kitchenalia. Today I had bread-boards carved with wheat-ears, wooden scoops and troughs, kitchen scales, china bowls banded with blue and white, and a wonderful old iron mangle I bought first thing this morning.

Now it was just before 9am and trade buyers, dealers who were not standing at this particular fair, were frowning and sucking their teeth over the stock on show. I was just deciding to return some of my empty boxes to my car when I was so peremptorily hailed.

I had never met the man before. I am not blonde. And I was about to move my estate car anyway.

How dare he, I seethed as I went out to my vehicle, brand me with a ridiculous nickname so publicly and so inaccurately. I couldn't help feeling sympathy for the little mouse of a woman he was watching unpack his boxes on the concrete floor.

Around 12.30 the fair entered the usual lunch time lull and I was glad of the chance to get a fellow dealer to keep an eye on my stall while I slipped off to the loo. As I queued in the ladies' line for the woeful facilities, blowing on my hands and rubbing them together to keep warm, I unwittingly listened to a conversation between two young men a few yards away.

They were giggling like schoolboys.

"Who's got it now?" asked one, grabbing some breath.

"Freddy from Berkshire," the other managed to tell him.

"Ol' Freddy? What did he get it for?"

"Three-fifty!"

They found this hilarious.

"It was fifty quid at seven this morning when Ian Green sold it to Bartie the Dog!"

This was nearly too much for them. They shushed each other's hoots of laughter and belatedly looked about to see if they had been overheard.

My queue moved up and, gratefully, I was able to get inside the brick block and out of the biting wind.

Back at my stall, I found the two young men had come to gossip with a stall-holder directly behind me. Seated on my folding chair, I eavesdropped comfortably while I ate my sandwiches and drank welcome hot coffee.

"Bartie sold it to Reg-with-the-leg for £85 at 8 o'clock and Reg got £120 for it from John and Linda from Barnsley. They flogged it to a bloke in a black hat for £175!" said one of the young men.

" ...and he did a deal," continued the other, "with the redhead who does the jewellery and bits and bobs. I don't know what she paid but she got £250 for it from Jacko Coles. He rushed it across to a bloke we don't know on the other side and he sold it to Freddy from Berkshire for £350!"

"Then," said the first one, with great glee, "Ol' Freddy bumped into us just now and said he'd just turned down £600 for it!"

They went off into peals of laughter again.

"Hang on," said the stall-holder directly behind me, warningly, "Customers."

I heard him enthusing about a pair of Oriental vases and his two friends took themselves off. His sales talk must have been successful because moments later there was that familiar rustle of goods being wrapped up.

During the early afternoon one of the friends came excitedly to report on progress.

"Ol' Freddy finally accepted £650!" he said. "And then the buyer was walking round with it under his arm when Rupert Thingy-Hyphen says in that posh accent of his, "I say! What have you got there?" The upshot is *he* lays paws to it for £750! Five minutes later, he flogged it to Winnie Pope - you know, the big fat bloke - for a grand!"

I counted on my fingers.

Someone called Ian, who brought the whatever-it-is with him to the fair, Bartie the Dog, Reg-with-the-leg, John and Linda, bloke in the black hat, the redhead with the jewellery, Jacko Coles, bloke we don't know, Ol' Freddy, an unknown buyer, Rupert with the hyphens, and Winnie Pope. That amounted to eleven times increasingly larger and larger sums had changed hands for this apparently highly desirable item.

I wondered what it was. I thought about the fellow who had it at the beginning. I thought he was unlikely to be delighted when he heard.

I sold the mangle. It was a nicely restored one with all the Victorian twiddly bits of cast iron picked out in black and gold. It went to an American with an open pick-up truck who drove off looking like a very up-market scrap dealer with my mangle, four early treadle sewing machines, a couple of enormous lead garden urns, and a life-size figure of Paris sticking up at the back.

There was a growing restlessness in our shed. Packing up early is severely frowned upon by the organisers, but rustling sounds from here and there indicated that some dealers were surreptitiously packing bits of stock to save time later when the fair officially closed.

The second of the friends came in hurriedly to tell the dealer behind me that the highly desirable item was on the move again.

"Winnie Pope got £1500 for it from some half-sharp looking old bloke dressed like a scarecrow!" he said. There was almost reverence in his voice.

Now, half-sharp is not a kind way to describe someone. In this district it means not all that bright. But it was a good description and I recognised the man as soon as he appeared in the shed. He had on the sort of tweeds that one's bespoke London tailor ran up for one or, in this case, possibly for one's father.

I saw at last that the object of such great desire was a clock.

It was mantelpiece sized, had brass finials and dainty brass feet, and its glossy inlaid body reminded me that women were once tight-laced into corsets.

The man in tweeds went from one dealer to another, enquiring, I imagined, if they were interested in buying the clock from him. He didn't offer it to me as the simplest person could see it was not what I dealt in, but he approached the dealer behind me.

The dealer paused from furtively wrapping his stock and looked the clock over with interest. Probably, like me, he was wondering why it had been the object of so much attention, not to mention cash.

It was nice enough. It had undoubtedly been a bargain at its original price.

"Been in the family for generations," said the old chap in tweeds, plummily but plaintively, "Hate to sell it, but you know how it is, death duties, the roof....... I'm getting on and the younger generation don't care for these things the way we do."

It was a touching story. I might have believed the old boy if I hadn't been in possession of inside information. I saw the dealer purse his lips as he turned the clock this way and that. He might have been trying not to laugh.

"I'm looking for two thousand five hundred, I'm afraid," the man in tweeds apologised sadly, sure the dealer was keenly interested, "I couldn't let it go for any less."

"Tell you what," said the dealer, "I'd love it, but I can't. I've just spent out on new stock. But see that fellow over there, I think he would be the one to talk to. His name's Ian Green."

I stood up for a better view.

Together, the dealer behind and I watched the old boy carry the clock across to the man who had called me Blondie. We gazed on avidly as the old fellow went through his routine about death duties and the roof and the uncaring younger generation.

When Ian Green yelled in fury, everyone stopped to watch.

The poor old chap backed nervously away from the abuse. Ian Green, becoming aware he was the focus of entertained attention, turned his reddened face to the other dealers and told them graphically what they could do to themselves.

Some of them returned to their surreptitious packing, hiding smiles. But the entertainment wasn't over.

The two friends appeared at the shed doors bringing between them a middle-aged Japanese gentleman. The Japanese gentleman cooed with undisguised pleasure as soon as he spotted the clock in the old fellow's arms. He nodded eagerly as the two friends did some fast talking and money and the clock changed hands for the last time that day.

The old chap in tweeds pocketed his gains and the two friends pocketed a commission on the sale.

Ian Green, who with the rest of us had witnessed the final sale of his clock, bellowed at the little mouse to get packed up and stormed out of the shed, away from grinning faces.

It was the dealer behind who coined a term for the clock.

The two friends came over to share their triumph.

"Where did you find the Japanese chap?" he asked them.

"Oh, we didn't," chortled one.

"He saw the clock earlier when Winnie had it and was looking for the old boy he sold it to," said the other, innocently, "So we helped him."

"What did he give for it?"

"Four grand."

The dealer whistled. I glanced at my wristwatch. It was just three o'clock.

"Eight hours, thirteen buyers, and an 800% per cent mark-up," I remarked.

"I thought you'd been listening," he said, "You should be pleased. It couldn't have happened to a nicer fellow."

I agreed it couldn't.

"What about the Japanese man?" I asked.

"He's a very happy man. He'll be on a flight back to Tokyo tonight," said one of the friends, "He thinks he can get double for it back home."

"Wait till I tell my wife about the eight-hour clock!" chuckled the dealer, "She doesn't like Ian Green either."

Nice Lions

Vincent thumped down the last plastic box behind the stall. The thud resounded in the hall. Echoes bouncing off the metal columns went twanging through the high iron arches bracing the roof.

Heads came up inquisitively to see if there was an expensive breakage they could be glad was not theirs.

The box contained only brassware. Unlike the piece of fine Meissen Vincent's partner, Keith, following behind, so carefully carried, it could be treated robustly.

Heads turned back to the task of setting out their own stock.

Keith, with an armful of delicate porcelain petals and cherub's tiny fingers to worry about, stepped aside to let two furniture dealers go by with an Edwardian wardrobe between them.

"Right," Vincent said, his eyes already roving over items being unwrapped on nearby stalls, "I'll scoot round while you set up."

"Right," said Keith, neatly arranging their table cover so the front drop would conceal their stock boxes.

They had fallen into their Antiques Fairs' routine years ago. Vincent always looked round while everyone was setting up. Keith always arranged their stock on the stall. Vincent liked to mosey round with his eyes flicking and assessing, weighing up the items, thinking of the price he could get if he saw something he liked the look of, thinking of the price he would be prepared to pay. He was good at it. Keith was adept at displaying the stock. He resented it if Vincent interfered.

"Morning, Keith," someone called out to him.

"Oh! Hello, Veronica dear, how are you?" Keith answered sociably. He had been so involved with his display he had hardly noticed the large lady setting up on his left. "I'm half asleep this morning!"

Veronica, immaculately tailored and coiffured, was moving glittering rings and heavy gold chains from a rigid briefcase with combination locks. She smiled at Keith across glass display cases from which padlocks dangled.

"How's Vincent?" she asked, "Left you to do the stall again, has he?"

"It's best, dear," Keith confided, "He was in such a mood in the van!

Anyway, he hasn't got the touch. Oh, look, and here's Moira. Hello, dear. That's a nice lion. Spelter is it?"

"Hello, Keith, love. You're doing your stall lovely again," responded the stall-holder on Keith's right. A lady of comfortable middle years with an overgrown perm like spaniel's ears, Moira was taking forever, as usual, to get set up.

Her stall was presently a welter of scrunched-up carrier bags and wads of newspaper from which intriguing noses, tails, handles, and spouts peeped out.

She looked critically at a dark metal shape, a lion couchant upon a marble plinth, deep in a crumpled nest of the Evening News. It was hardly recognisable as a lion for the dirt which had firmly set in every fold and crevice.

"No, love," she said, "I don't think it's spelter. It's a bit heavy for it."

Keith carefully added an exquisite porcelain dish to a tapering mahogany display stand and wandered over to look more closely at the lion.

"Pity there isn't a pair," he said and began to turn back to his work.

"The other one's under the stall," said Moira over her shoulder, divesting a naked parian figure of the modesty of its Daily Mail.

Keith spun back too eagerly. He checked and made himself relax.

Through the back of her head Moira felt his quickened interest. She had not been a dealer for twenty years without developing that sharp sixth sense for the right sort of genuine interest. The type that meant the handing over of cash.

She set aside the naked figure and began to peel two Sainsbury's carrier bags off a fancy brass trivet in severe need of Brasso.

"Is it in the same condition?" asked Keith, casually.

"Oh, yes, love," said Moira, calmly, "Filthy, but no damage. I'll get it for you."

Keith regarded the pair of grimy lions. Two emotions spiralled through him. One was a thrilling certainty that the lions were something special, the other a gleeful urge to show Vincent he could buy well, too.

He suppressed any show of eagerness, examined them only cursorily. If he could get them cheaply enough he could check them out later. If they were nothing special he could cover his costs, maybe make a small profit. If they really were something special he might do very well with them.

"What have you got on them?" he asked casually.

"I don't really know, love. What do think I should ask? Go on, make me an offer!"

Keith hated that. It made him feel so exposed. Too low and she'd laugh, too high and Vincent would kill him. He took the plunge.

"How would sixty-five do?"

Moira considered. Sixty-five pounds in the hand meant being able to tax her van at the end of the month. Hanging on for more might mean no sale, an illegal van, beans on toast, and her George getting at her by being sweetly uncomplaining in that needling way of his.

"Okay, love," she said. It was a reasonable profit margin, after all.

The lions had come with a lot of china from a house clearance George had done a few weeks ago. They had got the job cheap because of the state of the house, but a little bit of dirt never bothered George and Moira.

A willowy, ethereal, black-haired creature was drifting from stall to stall. She wore long drooping black and could have appeared in any vampire film. She needed only dry-ice vapour about her ankles. Cecily always looked as if she could do with a pint or two of blood, but her bank balance was healthy enough. She dealt, surprisingly, in architectural salvage, especially monumental garden ornaments, and 18th and 19th century bronzes.

She homed in on the lion from three stalls away. Keith was working on the mane with an old toothbrush from his cleaning kit.

"What a pity there isn't a pair," she sighed.

Keith looked up from his task.

"The other one's under the stall," he said.

"Is it in the same condition?"

Keith's heart began to beat faster. It always did when he knew he had a live one.

"Would you like to see it, dear? I haven't cleaned it yet."

Cecily made a small moue with her red lips and fluttered the long fingers of her right hand. The heavy ring she wore, with its enormous ruby dark as congealed blood, looked impossibly massive for her narrow white wrist to support in mid-air. Her hand dropped to the black folds at her breast.

"If it's no trouble," she said in her quiet unemphatic voice, delicately lowering densely blackened lashes over her alert eyes.

Hefting the lion Keith had not yet cleaned, she turned it over to check the bottom. Keith wondered deliriously if she did that to the vast garden ornaments she sold. Cecily handled the heavy lion on its marble base effortlessly.

"What's your best price?" she asked.

Keith pulled a figure out of the air.

"Three sixty-five," he said confidently.

Cecily put her head on one side, considering this. Keith put the other lion on his chair and made a business of indifference, rearranging a cup and saucer minutely on the mahogany stand. He had decided not to budge on the price. Cecily had not immediately put down the lion or countered his price with a lower figure. He was close to victory. Close, but not yet victorious.

His heart hammered away. He adjusted the position of an Art Nouveau vase.

"You'll take a cheque?" Cecily asked, ingenuously.

Keith managed to look regretful.

Cecily gave him a tiny rueful smile and put down the lion.

Keith's heart drummed a tight syncopation in his chest.

Producing a wallet, Cecily counted out large and small denomination notes onto Keith's table cover and picked up the cleaned lion from Keith's chair. Keith's heartbeat finished on a roll and slowed towards normal.

"I'll send Tony for the other one," she said and flowed away with the lion cradled on one arm like a lap dog.

Vincent, his holdall practically empty for there had been hardly a thing in the whole place with any profit left in it he wanted to buy, passed Cecily on his way back to Keith.

Nice lion, he thought, pity there isn't a pair.

"Just seen Cecily with a bronze lion," he remarked to Keith. He idly shifted a small cranberry glass dish from one side of a copper jug to the other.

"Oh," said Keith, very casually, replacing the cranberry glass dish in its original position, "Nice, was it?"

"Very," said Vincent, turning a Meissen candelabra slightly to the right, "Pity there wasn't a pair."

Keith turned the Meissen candelabra back, stood back to look at it, decided he preferred it the way Vincent had it, and twisted it to the right again.

"There was," he said, "There is."

Vincent looked at him warily, not sure if Keith was having him on.

"You had them?" he demanded.

Keith smirked.

"Where's the other one?" said Vincent urgently.

"Under the stall. She's sending that gorilla of hers back for it," said Keith, enjoying himself. Vincent was jealous, he decided, just because *he* hadn't done the deal.

Vincent pulled out the un-cleaned lion. He looked up at Keith with a frown.

"Where did you get them?" he asked, grudging respect in his voice.

Keith told Vincent where he got them. He told him how much he paid.

"That all?" Vincent exclaimed and laughed.

Cold doubt slithered up Keith's backbone.

Vincent turned the lion over, just as Cecily had done.

"I wish I'd seen them together," he said, "Solid bronze. Early, too. Lovely! Fancy you spotting them in amongst Moira's old junk! Go on then, what did you get for them?"

Vincent was smiling.

Keith's heart began to hammer again.

He was distracted from his answer by someone stopping by the stall. It was a humourless young man. Tattoos on his shaved head and bare arms declared his rage at society, a new twist on body language. He was wearing a denim waistcoat which had been ruggedly converted from a jacket by ripping off its sleeves.

"Cec'ly says you got a lion fing for her. Already paid for," said the young man. He glared at the lion in Vincent's hands. "That it?"

Vincent surrendered the lion.

The young man looked Vincent up and down and stared hard at Keith. Their very existence was an offence to him. Keith and Vincent could see that quite clearly. Disdainfully, he strutted away.

"Well?" urged Vincent, turning back to Keith, "How much did you get?"

"What would you have asked?" Keith countered cockily. Much more cockily than he felt.

"Oh, about seven fifty, eight hundred - maybe even a bit more if I really tried," Vincent said with a shrug and a grin.

It was not in Keith to lie to Vincent, much as he would have liked to at this moment. He miserably told him the figure he had asked.

Vincent's eyes seemed to grow until they looked frighteningly insecure in their sockets. With furiously compressed lips, he turned his back.

Keith knew it was no good telling himself he had just made three hundred quid for them in twenty minutes. If Vincent ever spoke to him again, he was never going to hear the last of it. Vincent was going to be impossible to live with. Keith wished he didn't have to ride home with him in the van.

Keith went to the front of the stall and began painstakingly to change his display round. He needed something to do, anything, just so he did not have to stand next to Vincent.

After a few minutes he realised Vincent was no longer fuming behind the stall. He had gone off somewhere. It was not much of a relief, but it was some.

On both sides of Keith his fellow stall-holders, unaware of the tiff, were talking to customers. He watched them wrapping up goods. Veronica in violet tissue-paper and smartly printed little bags; Moira in torn newspaper and creased carrier bags bearing the names of every supermarket and chain-store in the country. He did not even have a customer.

Normally an early three hundred profit like this would have buoyed him up for the day, making all his other sales that much easier, but he could only feel depressed about it. His little triumph was ashes.

"I know this is terribly bad form," murmured an unemphatic voice, "but I have to ask you a favour."

Cecily, drooping apologetically, stood before Keith's stall. The young man in the denim and skin slogans stood beside her, his mouth in a sneer, a bronze lion under each arm.

Keith looked at Cecily blankly, wondering what on earth she wanted.

"It's cash-flow, you see. I've just seen some fantastic statuary and, well, he wants cash. I wondered if I could persuade you to accept a cheque after all. Plus a little extra for inconvenience, naturally. Say another ten?"

Keith still looked blank. It was shock.

"Otherwise," said Cecily, a careful vagueness in her voice, "I'm afraid I would have to suggest you take the lions back. I must have the cash, you see. I'm sure you understand."

There was the slightest twitch from her minder. Along with the sneer, his face looked unhealthily eager.

Keith weighed up his options, such as they were. His heart had started its old tricks again.

He sighed and looked disconsolate.

"I don't take cheques, dear, you know how it is," he said.

With some alarm he saw the minder's sneer upturn into a ghastly smile.

Cecily sadly lowered her black lashes.

"Oh, dear," she said, "In that case we'll have to ask you to take your lions back."

"I know, dear," said Keith, ruefully, "But it's not really right, is it?"

"I do hate unpleasantness......," Cecily began, and the minder leaned forward.

"Oh, so do I, dear," said Keith hastily, "So do I. What say I keep a little tiny handling fee for goodwill, dear? Twenty per cent?"

Cecily looked amused.

"Seventy-three pounds? A touch outrageous, don't you think?"

Keith's heart was rattling in his chest.

"So is what you're asking me for, dear," he said, "I wouldn't want to fall out with you, and I'm sure you wouldn't want to fall out with me."

He took his wallet from inside his jacket. The fifty-pound notes were in there. The smaller notes were in a zipped trouser pocket.

"Tell you what, dear, here's three hundred and we'll call it quits.

"Shall I sort 'im, Cec'ly?" enquired the minder hopefully.

"No, Tony, not this time." Cecily made sure Keith saw the pale hand bearing the blood-dark stone rest in light restraint on her minder's arm. "Just gently pass him his lions. I may want to do business with him again."

Keith, hoping she would not notice his trembling hands, gave her the three hundred pounds and watched her black figure drift out of sight into the crowd with her thug flexing his decorated muscles in her wake.

Vincent, still in a huff, returning to get himself a hot coffee from their thermos found Veronica hovering anxiously over Keith, offering him a reviving pull on the contents of a silver hip flask. Late Georgian, or just possibly William IV, Vincent thought.

"Keith?" said Vincent, worriedly, "You all right? What's happened?"

"He's had a little run-in with that Cecily and her pet psychopath," clucked Veronica. Keith sat on his chair looking pale but triumphant. Shaken but surviving. The bronze lions on their marble plinths lay side by side on the floor beneath him.

"You've got the lions back," said Vincent in wonder.

"And sixty-five quid!" said Keith, rallying.

"But that's what you ...."

"I know," agreed Keith, managing a grin and a wink, "Now let's see what *you* can get for them!"

Custom Cars

The crunch of wheels on gravel had Archie Bond putting on his distance glasses to see who was parking at the side of the shop.

Twisting round in his office chair, he called through the archway to his wife, "Only a Metro, Lydia."

"Oh," replied Lydia. All the information needed by two people who have lived and worked together for as many years as she and Archie was in that one syllable. She disappeared to cut some sandwiches for their lunch.

The young couple who had arrived in the Metro pushed open the door of the shop setting a small bell jangling on its spring.

Taking a timid look round at beautifully polished pieces of mahogany and rosewood furniture and gazing upon the pictures, fine porcelain and exquisite glass, they saw through an archway the back of a plump man in shirtsleeves engrossed in paperwork at an old-fashioned bureau. He did not acknowledge them. They could hear the sound of a radio in a back room somewhere and the clatter of dishes.

They left again.

Lydia came through to put tea and sandwiches on Archie's desk.

"Did they buy anything?"

"No," said Archie with a snort, "Waste of time."

"Well," said Lydia, succinctly. She gave a tiny shrug of one shoulder. They both nodded, understanding was complete.

Archie had just finished his sandwiches when a Jaguar pulled in.

He called out to alert Lydia.

"No," he amended, seeing the number plate more clearly, "Forget it. It's five or six years old. Oh, wait a minute, there's a Merc just behind it." He peered deeply. "Yes. It's a new one!"

He smoothed his thinning hair and put on the blazer with polished buttons that hung on the back of his chair. He rolled the desk cover down to conceal the plate and crumbs and noted who emerged from the Mercedes.

The pussy-cat bow of her blouse tidied to her satisfaction at the neck of her collarless jacket, Lydia slid her sandwich plate into a drawer of her own dainty mahogany desk and took up an auction catalogue. Looking up from it with a practised smile as three people came in on each others' heels, she bade them all an equally pleasant, "Good afternoon."

She did not yet know which was which.

Ready with the twinkling smile he reserved for the right sort of person, Archie waited a few moments before he approached his customer.

Now Lydia knew. She rose to stand neutrally available for enquiries.

She briefly regarded the owners of the no-longer-new Jaguar. They were a middle-aged couple, presently discussing, *sotto voce*, a pair of seascapes in oils.

Think this is a museum, thought Lydia, a way to pass the afternoon.

The young woman who had driven the Mercedes was looking over a chinoiserie cabinet with a thoroughness which suggested she could be a dealer. Archie liked to know that straight off.

"Good day, ma'am," he said, "I can see you know what you are looking at. It is an excellent example of its kind. Would you, by any chance, be in the antiques trade yourself?"

She looked up, smiled with amusement at the suggestion, and shook her head.

This was as Archie had hoped. A wealthy customer was much more welcome to him than another dealer looking to pare his margins to the bone for their own profit.

"If there is anything I can tell you about the cabinet, please don't hesitate to ask, anything at all," said Archie.

The woman gave him another smile, a brief one, and went on with her examination of the cabinet. She opened and closed the many small drawers, looking carefully inside each.

Archie examined his customer.

She was tall, had straight fair hair brushed back and neatly fixed by a tortoiseshell slide at the nape of her neck. She wore an unadorned fitted black jacket with black trousers and polished low-heeled shoes. A small black bag hung on a long strap from one shoulder. Since she had removed only her right leather glove, holding it in her still-gloved left hand, Archie could not immediately determine if she wore a wedding ring. He assembled all the clues available to him and sought to place her in context.

A second wife, he conjectured, of a rather older husband. Very sure of herself. Probably has her every whim gratified. Good with the step-children, has none of her own yet. Has staff to help run a big house. Obviously looking for a striking piece for the dining room, or perhaps the entrance hall.

He was about to offer her information about the cabinet, a preliminary to closing the certain sale, when his customer moved on to another item. She proceeded to give a rosewood davenport the same close scrutiny she had given the chinoiserie cabinet.

Archie gave Lydia a look with an optimistically raised eyebrow. Lydia raised both.

Yes, she thought, the young woman just might take both items.

Lydia pictured her at home in high-ceilinged rooms with tall windows. Dressed with expensive simplicity, she would soon be telling her dinner-guests about her exciting finds at Bond's Antiques just behind the High Street.

Lydia cast a glance towards her little mahogany desk with the Italian lamp casting a warm glow over the telephone, credit card machine, and the silver salver on which a fan of their business cards was arranged. There was a magazine in the drawer she was longing to get back to. If it was only the Jaguar people there, she would have. Instead she watched Archie.

He was enthusing about the davenport, demonstrating the clever rise and fall mechanism. The young woman nodded, occasionally smiled, listened patiently and then moved away to the huge Georgian break-front bookcase that had been in the shop for two years. Lydia told Archie when he bought it that it wouldn't sell. It was far too big for nowadays. It would be just wonderful if the Mercedes woman finally took it off their hands.

As Lydia tried to interpret the demeanour of their customer, the Jaguar people left the seascapes and approached her.

Lydia fixed a smile, prepared to break the bad news to them politely.

"£800, I'm afraid."

The couple turned to consult with each other. Lydia turned away to watch the more exciting action across the room. Archie was telling his customer about Georgian craftsmanship.

The Jaguar couple exchanged meaningful minute grimaces, little shrugs and small angled head movements.

The man drew Lydia's attention back by touching her arm.

"We'll pop back," he said.

Lydia barely bothered to nod. Along with, "We'll think about it," this was a common phrase that meant only one thing. No sale.

The little bell over the door bounced and jangled and they were gone.

Archie ran a finger inside his collar. He had worked hard, giving of his knowledge, but his customer, listening with apparent great interest to his every word, had contributed nothing but nods and occasional smiles. His questions about what she was looking for, where a piece would be expected to go, what style she currently lived with, had elicited no more than a wince and a uncertain shrug. Now she was looking at her wristwatch and glancing around at the rest of the furniture, a sweeping gaze that found nothing it wanted to settle on.

"No doubt you will wish to think about the items you've seen," said

Archie, trying to keep desperation out of his tone, "Probably you will need to consider back at home just whether the bookcase would fit in. Or the davenport.........."

The fair young woman gave a short soft laugh and Archie paused.

"Not really," she said.

Archie maintained a near-smile from habit. The voice was all wrong.

Lydia heard it, too. Her illusion of the mansion, the dinner party guests, fell away.

"I just wondered what all the fuss was about," said the young woman, waving a hand round the shop, "I thought I'd have a look for meself."

She checked her watch again.

"Gotta go. Thanks for the chat and all that."

The bell jangled and the door closed behind her.

Archie and Lydia exchanged heated voluble looks.

"Are you sure she was in the Mercedes?" snapped Lydia.

They both pushed through to the office.

"There!" Archie was indignant in his vindication.

There was the gleaming Mercedes, this year's top of the range model.

They watched her get in, fasten her seat belt, and pull on her right hand glove.

They both saw her settle the hard black cap with its shiny peak on her sleek fair head, completing her chauffeur's uniform. The engine purred into life. The Mercedes was expertly driven away.

Archie and Lydia Bond communicated silent fury. After a moment something else outside registered on Lydia. In surprise she said, "Archie, the Jaguar's still there."

"I thought they'd gone," said Archie.

"I didn't take much notice," said Lydia, "but the man did say he'd pop back. The pair of seascapes. £800. They've gone to the bank!"

Archie smoothed his thin hair and gave his blazer a straightening tug. Lydia adjusted her pussy-cat bow. She looked past Archie at the sound of crunching gravel.

"It's a Porsche," she said, "A couple of years old, mind, so don't get your hopes up."

"It's personalised number plates that throw me," grumbled Archie.

Looking at each other with knowing raised eyebrows, they put their smiles in place and stepped through to the shop.

The Green-Room Chaise-Longue

Eight year old Mattie had seen a ghost. He never told anyone. He hugged the experience to himself and forgot about it by the time he grew up.

"I have 35, ... 35, ...40 pounds, 45 ....50 ... 55..." The auctioneer's eyes flickered over the assembly for increased bids.

A sharp oily smell of damp raincoats pervaded the half-empty room. The heavy grey downpour still splashing at the windows and clattering on the corrugated metal roof was undoubtedly responsible for the small turnout at the sale of the old theatre's fixtures, fittings, and props.

Matthew Bowen was quite happy about the poor attendance. He had already successfully bid for the costume baskets. Twenty of them sold as one lot! He could hardly believe his luck. The only other bidder had quickly lost interest so they went for a wonderfully low price.

Now Matthew was after a big box of assorted table lamps. Most were electric but a couple were genuine Victorian oil-lamps dating from the theatre's hey-day in the 1890's. The theatre had continued to flourish long into the twentieth century. Matthew remembered the lamps being used as props in a production of 'The Importance of Being Earnest', nearly twenty years ago, when from the wings he had watched his own young mother play Cecily. Since then the old theatre had declined and finally closed.

"...55...55.... thank you, all done at 55. Mr. Bowen, isn't it?"

Matthew nodded. It impressed him that the auctioneer had his name down pat after a single earlier successful bid. Euphoric over his purchase of the lamps, Matthew imagined them cleaned up for sale in his shop. Just one of the oil-lamps would more than cover this afternoon's expenses.

"Ladies and gentleman, at the back we have Lot 66, a chaise-longue, probably late 19th century, mahogany frame. One for the upholsterers among you....." The auctioneer paused for the inevitable laugh from his audience.

The chaise-longue's velvet cover was undeniably in a sorry state.

Horse-hair poked through at the edges and the prolapsed springs and webbing in their hessian covering touched the floor. Dust puffed from the velvet when the auction-room porter jovially slapped the padded head-rest.

"One hundred pounds? Who'll start me off at one hundred pounds?"

There was shuffling but no-one bid.

"Oh, you must have this one," said a voice very softly behind Matthew.

He guardedly glanced over his shoulder, but he couldn't tell who had spoken, or who the remark was addressed to. He didn't think it could be meant for him. The faces of the handful of people behind him were expressionless, intent. He settled his scarf closer, pulling it up a bit at the back to cover his neck better. He wished they would heat the place on miserable days like this.

"Fifty pounds," said the auctioneer, "Do I hear fifty pounds?"

"It's very reasonable," said the voice behind Matthew. Matthew decided it wasn't speaking to him and didn't look round. He didn't need to be told it was very reasonable. He was waiting for someone else to start the bidding. So, apparently, was everyone else.

"Ladies and gentlemen," chided the auctioneer, "a late-Victorian, mahogany-framed chaise-longue, with original brass casters!"

There was another small laugh for his heart-broken tones. He grew brisk.

"Come on now, someone start me at thirty pounds!"

"You do it," said the voice.

Matthew gave a little shiver. He watched the auctioneer scanning the room and waited for the bid from whoever behind him was being urged to make it.

"Twenty-five!" said a man near the front, raising his catalogue.

"Thank you, sir! I have 25...25..."

"For goodness sake, you're going to lose it!" said the voice behind Matthew. He wondered why on earth the owner of the voice didn't do its own bidding if it was so keen on the chaise-longue.

Not unexpectedly, even after such a reluctant start, the bidding rose rapidly to seventy-five pounds. Matthew entered a bid of eighty pounds just as the auctioneer was about to sell to the man with the catalogue.

"About time, too!" said the voice. Matthew frowned. Another late bid was apparently about to come from behind him.

The man at the front waved his catalogue.

"Eighty-five, thank you," said the auctioneer. He turned back to Matthew expectantly.

Matthew nodded.

"Ninety," said the auctioneer and looked to the man with the catalogue for more. The man shook his head.

"Ninety pounds....." The auctioneer looked around for any new bids. "Any advance on ninety pounds?"

Matthew prepared for the bid from behind that must come now. All right, he thought, I can go to a hundred and twenty, but I must not get carried away. A hundred and twenty is my *absolute* limit.

"Ninety pounds! Sold to Mr. Bowen for ninety pounds! Lot 67, an umbrella stand............."

Adrenalin was still coursing in Matthew's veins. The chaise-longue was his!

He turned round, expecting to see someone furious with a companion for failing to enter the bidding at all. The people behind him seemed perfectly calm. No-one looked cross or sheepish.

Matthew sniffed. He had been aware for a while of vague smell that had nothing to do with dank raincoats or dusty lots. Sweet, but faint, some kind of scenty smell, he thought, and then found the last traces of it had gone. He decided, as he made his way from the room, that it was probably furniture polish.

The rain ceased as Matthew queued to settle his bill in the auctioneer's office. By the time he fetched his battered old van and began to load his purchases the sun was out and the temperature had risen quite a few degrees. He sweated inside his waxed jacket as he man-handled the chaise-longue into his van. The mahogany frame was heavy and he had difficulty keeping the sagging upholstery out of the wet. Everywhere dripped.

"Just like being on tour," said the voice he had heard in the auction room, in pleased tones. It was a woman's voice, but with gravel in it.

With the chaise-longue half into the back of the van and drops still splashing from the roof, Matthew was in no position to see who was speaking.

"I used to enjoy touring," mused the voice.

"Oh, yes?" panted Matthew, sure he was being addressed this time.

He became aware of that sweet smell again, a flowery, powdery, sort of aroma. It must be the scent she was wearing.

It irritated him that she spoke from behind him instead of standing where he could see her. He could not look over his shoulder at this point in his struggle with the chaise-longue without risking himself an injury.

The heat of the sun in the clearing sky was burning hot on his neck. Despite this, a little chillly frisson rippled across his back hairs.

A sudden rivulet of rain-water ran off the van's roof onto his head and straight into his eyes. Matthew gave vent to a furious strangled noise of protest, shutting his eyes tight, and blindly heaved the chaise-longue the last few feet aboard. He hunted in his pockets for a handkerchief and wiped his face.

His companion had gone. She could be any one of several women helping to load other vehicles around him. Matthew didn't care. He just wanted to get his things on the van and go home.

His euphoria had died away and he was already wondering if he had really bought well. Twenty costume baskets that no-one else wanted and a tatty chaise longue, he thought. Had he suffered a bout of auction fever?

He went to get his box of lamps and recovered his senses. There was nothing wrong with the oil-lamps that brass polish couldn't fix and original early electric lighting was very much in vogue just now. Baskets were perennially popular, and even the chaise-longue would make him a good return when it had been restored.

His new possessions tucked round with blankets, Matthew slammed his back doors, swiftly side-stepping a final cascade of rain-water from the dented roof, and wedged himself into the driver's seat. He strapped in two baskets on the passenger seat that wouldn't fit in the back, fastened his own seat-belt, and wound down his rain-speckled window so he could see out to his right.

The elderly van's engine fired quite happily on the turn of the key but the clutch-pedal, as always, fought back all the way until the last quarter-inch. It came up abruptly under Matthew's boot and the van jerked forward, bouncing over pot-holes full of water, to the yard gates.

"Oops!" came a voice faintly from the back.

Matthew's eyes widened. Hairs stood up thoroughly this time all the way down his back. He looked automatically in the interior mirror, but that was useless. A big sheet of plywood installed behind the van's seats blocked off the rear.

In his wing mirrors, Matthew saw two Volvo estates of vastly different vintage were in convoy right behind him. He shook himself. It must have been someone outside, he thought, probably mocking him. Winding up his window again, he turned on the radio. At the gates he waited for a gap in the traffic on the main road, jolted out, turned right, and drove uneventfully home.

A friend helped him unload on the promise of beer and pizza. They ate upstairs in Matthew's living quarters over the shop, actually a bare storage space with extremely basic facilities, and Matthew saw him out and locked up downstairs as the sun was slipping down behind the lock-up shops across the road and the sky deepened to evening.

He had an urge to play with his favourite new acquisitions, to look them over possessively, reassure himself he had done well. He didn't bother fighting his way through his crowded stock to the light switches at the back of the shop.

He could see well enough as he edged between the stacked costume baskets to the big box of lamps beside the chaise-longue.

Kneeling, Matthew reached out to take hold of the box to carry it upstairs.

Every single hair on his body stood on end. This time she was in front of him. Matthew's mouth went dry. He breathed in her sweet scent with his mouth open in a gasp.

She wasn't very clear, but he could make out that she was sitting very upright on the frayed velvet.

"Errg," he said weakly in the back of his throat. She tilted her head enquiringly.

"I won't be staying, dear," she said, "I made up my mind years ago you should have it. You were a good boy. Never told a soul, did you? Because if you had someone might have put two and two together. Might have had a good look. Poor Oscar! Thank goodness all that sort of thing doesn't matter any more."

Matthew, speechless, goggled.

She stood up, an indistinct shape now among the shadows.

"I was Wardrobe, dear, no-one important, but I had a long life and I saw them all. Wonderful, it was. Except the way they treated poor Oscar. That's why I sewed it all into the Green-Room chez-long and guarded it all my days and after. Should be worth a bob or two now. So you have it, for being a good boy. Get yourself a new van, at least!"

Matthew heard her soft wheezing laugh fade away and knew he was alone. With darting glances, he checked all around himself anyway. The scent had faded away. too. Trembling, he stared into the fizzing dark at the chaise-longue.

It was his, bought publicly at auction. He had a receipt for it on the table upstairs.

Clambering across the solid frame and sagging velvet, Matthew threw himself, flailing, at the light switches and snapped on every one.

Standing bemused at the back of a London auction room, Matthew thought about the easy-going laughter under the corrugated roof of the auction-room back home. Here, amid the gilded plush, he could almost taste the tension.

The leather writing case initialled O.F.O.W.W. and the manuscripts he had discovered had just sold for figures that caused Matthew's eyes to glaze over while his mind went protectively numb. Now lot 22, the tattiest chaise-longue ever offered here was about to come under the hammer.

Matthew looked across rows of heads bobbing over catalogues to where it stood, practically disembowelled, behind the auctioneer's dais and suddenly he smelled flowery, powdery, scent in the air.

"Well, it is yours, dear, I suppose."

The soft gravelly voice behind him was sad.

Goose-flesh rippled along Matthew's spine. Hairs stood up on his arms. He ran.

He hurtled frantically past gilded chairs and turned heads.

"Ladies and gentlemen," the auctioneer announced smoothly a few moments later, "Lot number 22 in your catalogue has been withdrawn.
We move on now to Lot 23........."

"You're a good boy, Mattie," said the voice.

It was drifting away, faint as breeze in Matthew's ear, as he struggled to load the remains of his chaise-longue into his battered old van. There lingered just the merest redolence of something flowery and powdery in the dusty old velvet.

The Egyptian Cat

Miss Augusta Reed, a much-travelled lady and amateur archaeologist, had always believed strongly that when abroad one should eat what the natives ate and not make a fuss about it.

This had given her a robust constitution which, however, failed to save her from an outbreak of cholera during her last trip to North Africa. She died on the boat back to England and was buried at sea. This was exactly what she would have wanted.

Her three cabin trunks, folding table, camp bed, and pith helmet were delivered to the over-large town-house that was her English home.

Mary Hobbs, cook-housekeeper to Miss Reed, indeed her only staff, clutched her late mistress's pith helmet with its trailing veil to her ample bosom and sobbed loudly into a large handkerchief as the cabin trunks and other paraphernalia were carried into the hall.

When she had tipped the men and closed the door, she reverently laid the pith helmet on the largest trunk and retired to her kitchen to drink herself senseless on the late Miss Reed's late father's finest port.

Having an employer who was more frequently absent than present, Mary Hobbs had slipped unchecked into some rather bad habits.

In addition to working her way through the contents of the wine cellar, Mary Hobbs seldom, if she could avoid it, actually cleaned or cooked. Miss Reed, making notes or reading a book at the table, never noticed the dust or what she was given.

A regular order for foodstuffs in quantities for two persons and occasional visitors continued to be delivered by tradesmen every Friday even when Miss Reed was away. Mary Hobbs sold off the excess supplies at the back door but still grew very stout. She clothed herself from the late Miss Reed's late mother's wardrobe, the late Mrs. Reed having been of similar girth.

Mary was well-known at the Dog and Ferret, a few streets away, for willingly standing her round and singing with great gusto beside the piano.

Waking in her kitchen armchair some hours later with a bit of a head,

Mary found there was just a glass left in the bottle and poured it delicately out to take up to bed with her.

The trunks in the hall caused her to sigh sadly for poor Miss Reed, the best employer she could have wished for.

Placing her glass carefully on the hall table, and taking a hairpin from the unravelling bun at the back of her head, she opened the largest trunk. There was a nice bound box nestling among Miss Reed's travelling attire. Mary had it open in a moment.

Mary Hobbs was honest in her way. She never sold off the silver, for instance, even when she was quite tempted. To her mind perks were one thing, pilfering was quite another. So she took just one small item to remember Miss Reed by and because she fancied it.

It was a little Egyptian cat. Sitting up so straight and regal and wearing a necklace, it made Mary smile. It even had a ring in one ear like a sailor. She popped it into her apron pocket where it banged against her plump knees as she climbed the stairs with her night-cap glass of port.

At four the following afternoon, Mary Hobbs admitted Miss Reed's solicitor and heard that Miss Reed's heirs, cousins of the same name, would be moving into the house within the month. They would keep Mary on, he said, if they found her satisfactory.

When the new owners arrived on the appointed day at ten o' clock in the morning, Mary Hobbs was still in bed. They found unwashed dishes in the stone sink and empty port bottles on the kitchen table.

Mary Hobbs was awakened, sacked, and on the doorstep with her bags packed within the hour.

She moved into a lodging house. On the mantelpiece in her room she fondly placed the Egyptian cat and a bottle of port she had kept under her bed in case of emergency. Two weeks later she was thrown out for disturbing the peace of other lodgers and not paying her rent.

After sleeping out for a week or so she was rescued and found a bed in a mission hostel for fallen women. There she took up religion for something to do, since they didn't allow drinking, and became a suffragette.

She died whilst enthusiastically hitting a high C during a hymn at an open-air service in Hyde Park ten years later. By that time women had got the vote.

Mary Hobbs's belongings were raffled for charity.

The Egyptian cat was won by the owner of a tea-room just off Piccadilly who decided to redecorate the place with Egyptian motifs. For thirty years the Egyptian cat sat on a shelf behind the till. It was taken down when tea-rooms went out of fashion and coffee-bars came in.

The unwanted oddments and ornaments were taken away by a rag-and-bone man in cardboard boxes. These sat on the floor of his showroom, a poky shop on a corner site down a cobbled back-street, where he weighed and sorted old clothes brought in for half-a-crown a sackful.

Down the cobbled street one Autumn evening came a little party of revellers from a different part of town. The two men wore sports jackets and yellow cravats, the young women, high heels slipping on the cobbles, wore dresses frothing with petticoats. They peered through the grimy windows.

The man inside rubbed his fingerless mittens together as he eagerly welcomed them in. He took things from boxes, holding them up, urging the men to buy this or that item for the ladies.

"Oh, Gerry, that's cute!" one of the girls exclaimed, "Oh, do buy me the pussy cat!"

Good-naturedly, Gerry paid over five shillings and presented his escort with the Egyptian cat. When the other girl had a little present too, the four went laughing away.

After queuing in baking sun, thirteen-year-old Henry stepped with relief into the relative cool of the building. He carried an item he wanted to put before the experts from the Antiques Road Show.

"Now this is interesting," said the valuer, "Are you keen on Egyptology?"

Henry nodded.

"Well, this is a rather nice little Egyptian bronze figure of the cat goddess, Bastet, which the early Egyptians would certainly have regarded as a sacred object. How long have you had it?"

"Nearly all my life," said Henry, noticing for the first time that a TV camera on wheels had silently appeared right beside him. "My great-aunt Liz left it to me."

"When she died?"

"Oh, no," Henry assured him, "She's still alive. She went to live in Los Angeles. I was just a baby. My mother said she left it for me."

"Your mother's aunt? Is that right?"

"Yes," said Henry, adding helpfully, "Great-uncle Gerry bought the cat as a present for my great-aunt before they were married. In a junk shop." The wheeled camera swung round to be full on Henry's face as he talked.

"Well, I expect you'd like to know what your cat is really worth?"

That was not really what Henry wanted to know. He wanted to know if it had come from the tomb of a great pharaoh, he wanted to know all about Bastet, he wanted to know how his Bastet had come to be in back-street shop in London. He wanted history, not finance. But there was a long queue still waiting, so Henry just nodded.

"Well, your parents should increase their household contents insurance. At the right sale, your cat might fetch £3000!"

Henry looked appropriately stunned for the camera.

There was little more chat. The next-in-line was eager to sit in Henry's place. He made his way out of the crowded hall into the hot sunshine to ring his father from a phone box.

"Are we rich?" asked his father, laughing.

"Not bad. How long will you be, Dad?

"Be there in five. I just dropped off a fare."

Henry sat on a wall to wait, turning the Egyptian cat over and over in his hands.

He looked the taxi over critically as his father drew up and got out stretching widely to ease his back. Henry earned money cleaning their taxis and he took some pride in their appearance. The logos on the front doors were their advertisement. This cab was still looking okay.

"He was interested in the cat," said Henry, "He said it could fetch £3000 in the right sale and you should increase your insurance."

His father whistled, looking at the Egyptian cat with new respect.

"It's nice to know Aunt Liz gave you something so valuable. Come on, get in." His father slid back into the driver's seat. "We'll get home and you can tell your mother all about it. Do you think you'll be on TV?"

"I might be," said Henry, absently. He was staring thoughtfully at the Egyptian cat. "I can look up Bastet when we get home, but I don't suppose I'll ever find out how she got here."

He climbed into the passenger seat, pulled shut his door with the Reed's Taxis logo on the side, and fastened his seat belt.

Flying Pigs and the Arm of The Venus de Milo

Everyone needs a real holiday sometime. Antiques dealers find the concept difficult to grasp. What does an antiques dealer do on his or her day off? They go to an antiques fair.

Peter and Angela Marks had tried holidaying in Devon, Cornwall, Northumbria, and Weston-super-Mare. It didn't work. No sooner had they unpacked their bags than by some terrible magnetism and natural divining they would find the local antiques centre and home in on the area where all the little antiques and curio shops seem to cluster together for company. Having exhausted them, and themselves, they would buy the local paper and start in on the local fairs.

This year it was going to be different. Italy. Beautiful Architecture, Culture, Good Food, and plenty of Fine Wine.

Maybe in the pursuit of culture they might visit the odd museum, but mainly they would just relax and rediscover the art of conversation about something, anything, other than the antiques trade. Maybe pigs might fly.

The American on the aeroplane was a good conversationalist. He knew something about everything. As he chatted to his seat companion he moved effortlessly from sport to politics, philosophy to food, music to muscle-building, and was particularly expansive on the bargains he had acquired in every city of the world.

Peter drowsed over his book, but the drone of the American's not-uncultured accent in the seat behind kept Angela's attention distracted.
The words and pictures of her magazine were spilled meaninglessly before her eyes like so much Greek with ink splodges.

".....now in Stratford-upon-Avon I bought the most amazing ...."

Angela tried again. The in-flight magazine was concerning itself with the pleasures and treasures of Belgium. Pretty place.

"...just outside the Kremlin...I'd gotten the most wonderful ...."

Mediaeval Bruges. Lace.

".......it was a really good deal. Then in Madrid I bought ...."

Canal-side buildings. Chocolates.

"....imagine how I felt. .... offered me one of the actual arms of the Venus de Milo......."

Angela turned a page. Travel insurance.

"........paid cash - in dollars, naturally. Not a pair, of course, so......."

Competition for a case of champagne.

"Excuse me.....got to go visit the john."

Angela distinctly heard a sigh of relief behind her. She smiled.

The tannoy burbled with the relaxed confident voice of their pilot. Angela woke Peter to tell him he needed to fasten his safety belt. They were about to land.

Their first-floor hotel room overlooked the car-park but it was spacious and clean. Peter and Angela looked forward to lazing by the pool, exploring the locality just as far as feet and local transport would take them, and trying out as many of the local restaurants and bistros as possible during their ten-day stay.

By the second day, strolling back to their hotel late in the evening on warm cobbles between tall shuttered buildings after an excellent meal of fresh mussels, chicken in a wine sauce, a dessert of zabaglione, followed by coffee and brandy, they felt carefree and truly on holiday. The buzz of voices and laughter and the clink of glasses at pavement tables as they passed was a pleasure to hear. A sudden unrestrained and incomprehensible torrent of Italian coming from beyond a high courtyard gate where an unseen couple were furiously arguing seemed merely picturesque. It made Peter and Angela smile complacently at each as if they had never had a misunderstanding in their life. They were untroubled. Relaxed. Enjoying themselves.

Next morning things changed. The voice drifting up from the car-park to their open window demanded to know the whereabouts of someone called Eduardo. Angela peered down directly on to the heads of the American from the aeroplane and a shrugging individual with a broom. The man with the broom became animated with an eagerness to help when the American produced his wallet. He subsided and frowned hard when shown a mere photograph. Angela could see quite well that what the American held out was a picture of a statue.

"Eduardo?" the American asked again.

He finally cleared the deep frown from the face of the man with the broom by offering him a fistful of paper currency.

Angela watched the American disappear to follow the directions he was given. She understood only one word of the Italian directions he had received - the destination.

Shc turned slowly from the window, musing aloud, "Eduardo."

"Sorry?" said Peter, giving her an odd look.

"We need a car," she said.

"We do?"

"Oh, yes."

Map in hand, Angela navigated while Peter drove the hired Fiat.

"What was he driving?" asked Peter. A certain scepticism lingered, but his blood sang its old tune.

"Didn't see, but you can't miss him."

"No. Just a matter of keeping our ears open. I had great difficulty sleeping though him on the plane."

"You missed the important bit."

"Could be a wild goose chase."

"Left at the next junction and immediately right."

Peter swung the car left and right.

"You sure these are roads? They're just cobbled alleys. My teeth are rattling."

"Just keep straight on now, it should lead to open countryside."

Angela put aside the map, opened a guide book and traced her finger down the index.

"St. Paolo," she read aloud, "Partially ruined in the Second World War. Regular services held for the small local population. Open to the public on personal request of the priest. No charge is made but a small courtesy donation is customary."

The car bounced free of the bone-shaking cobbles and ran smoothly onto dusty tarmac between olive groves and undulating countryside with blue-hazed hills in the distance.

"Five miles. Nice views."

"What about money?"

"If Eduardo doesn't take travellers cheques, one of us can go back to town for cash."

"What would one do about import duty?"

"Simple enough. Declare it. Garden ornament - £50."

"Heavy though. Not exactly hand luggage."

"Ship it."

"What if it gets broken?"

They looked at each other and burst out laughing.

A shiny red Alfa Romeo was parked under trees at the side of the track that led up to the ruined monastery.

"The priest's?" suggested Angela

"Our friend's," said Peter, parking in the shade of a line of trees on the other side of the track.

"He's a bit out of our price range," said Angela doubtfully.

"I'd say he's borrowed it from a friend. Hire-cars are newer. That makes him cheaper than us. Let's find Eduardo."

"He's got to be the factotum around here or the Yank wouldn't have been asking a groundsman about him, " said Angela, "The hotel receptionist said an Eduardo worked there last year."

They started up the path to the monastery. Crumbling rose-coloured stone buildings, over which vines ran wild, stood charmingly on a low hill against a blue sky.

The chapel door stood wide open. They stepped into the cool dimness and waited for their eyes to adjust.

"`Open to the public on personal request of the priest,'" quoted Angela, "What priest?"

A soft snuffling, snorting, sound reached them. It terminated abruptly with a louder snort. A darker shape rose from the shadows of front pews. It swayed. Light from the doorway showed a glint of white at the throat.

"Nominae Patris.....et...........Filio Sancti....ummm," the dark figure mumbled and sat down again. After a moment the snoring began again.

"I think that constitutes consent," said Peter, "but our business must be further up the hill."

They toiled up the slope.

It was almost noon and very quiet except for busy insects and distant cockerels. Only the parked cars below and a plane, tiny in the blue overhead, reminded them it was the twentieth century. And the thumping music that suddenly erupted from one of the stone buildings as a door was flung open. It ceased abruptly and a young man emerged, trundling a venerable wooden-wheeled barrow across the yard. He halted and gave his visitors a wide smile of perfect teeth.

"£150 for that barrow back home," commented Peter.

Taking the blast of the dazzling smile, Angela muttered, "Any price you care to name for Eduardo back home."

Peter gave a resentful grunt.

The young man addressed them in Italian, confirming that he was indeed Eduardo.

Angela did her best with the few words she had mastered but he interrupted with another megawatt smile.

"English? I know a little. We speak English. You want to see over the monastery? I show you. The priest is old. This way, please."

"The priest is drunk," muttered Peter trailing behind. He paused at the building Eduardo had just emerged from. Eduardo looked round like a shepherd anxious to keep the flock together and hastened back to close the door.

"The dog," he said, "she will get out. She is having little dogs."

Peter smiled to show he accepted this lie. It wasn't any dog he had glimpsed in there.

Eduardo clearly like to practice his English. He practised it at length as he showed Peter and Angela over the ruins.

"You are on holiday? You enjoy it here in Italy, yes? Is not too hot for you? I was in England for a little while - in Birmingham. Nice place. The people very friendly. Is more modern than St. Paolo but not so warm. Fine big buildings. Many businesses. I stayed with my uncle there. He work for undertakers. Like my father and my brother."

"Eduardo," interrupted Angela, "We are antiques dealers. Do you have antiques to sell?"

Eduardo widened his smile and spread his hands. He indicated the crumbling stone monastery, the tiled courtyard and his wooden wheel-barrow, encompassed the surrounding fields and groves of olive trees and produced a slow shrug of his shoulders right up to his ears.

Peter closed his eyes with a pained sigh and looked away. Innocent son of the soil helping out an elderly priest be buggered, he thought.

Angela pursed her lips and gave Eduardo a friendly look of complete disbelief.

"Maybe a few things, here and there," Eduardo conceded, "I could ask around for you."

"Has the American been here?" asked Angela, "Today?"

"No. No American has come here today." Eduardo looked defeated. He had told the truth and it was only just after midday.

"Well, who does the red car down there belong........" Angela did not bother to finish the question. Eduardo's pride was transparent. It was his.

"Okay," said Peter, checking his watch. He nodded to Angela.

"Let's get on with it."

"How much are you asking for it?" Angela asked.

"My car?" Eduardo was genuinely puzzled.

"No," said Angela, patiently, "The arm of the Venus de Milo."

"Oh," said Eduardo, nodding, "The arm for the American. If you want it you must pay me much."

He stared into space for a moment before naming a figure in lira.

Peter took out a pocket calculator, punched buttons, and showed the displayed figure to Angela who laughed.

"You want to see the arm I have for the American?"

Angela said they did.

"You wait," he said, taking up the handles of the wheel-barrow, "I bring it."

He returned with a long sacking package on his barrow. He made sure to close the outbuilding door carefully.

"How's the dog?" asked Peter.

"Fine," said Eduardo, firmly, "She does nicely. You want a pup?"

"I might," said Peter with a grin. He slid the sacking back and examined the exposed marble hand and forearm. He peered at the other end. He checked the hand against his own.

"A left hand," he said, "So the American already has a right?

Eduardo shrugged.

"Now we have a sensible discussion about the price," said Peter.

Ten minutes later they paid Eduardo just under his original price. Eduardo found no difficulty accepting a traveller's cheque. Peter produced the car keys and Eduardo, whistling cheerfully, wheeled his barrow away to the hired Fiat.

"Quick," said Peter to Angela, pulling open the door of the outbuilding as soon as Eduardo was out of sight round the corner, "Take a look."

Angela looked. Peter pulled the door shut again and taking her arm hurried her after Eduardo.

"Amazing," she murmured.

"Were you born here in St. Paolo?" asked Peter, taking leave by the hired car.

Eduardo said he was. He lived here with his mother and father, older brother and four sisters. He was the youngest of his family. He wheeled his barrow back up the slope.

"Okay," said Angela, after a swift conference with Peter, "Now we are just unwary tourists."

Peter drove the hired Fiat back along the road about a mile, turned the car to face away from the road under the shade of a tree and raised the hatchback's rear door. He took out their lunch of prosicuito, tomatoes, olives, grapes, cheese, and local bread and wine, and arranged the sacking parcel to advantage.

It was very quiet, being still lunch-time, and the road was deserted. Under the sheltering tree they ate, drank, and waited.

The American drove by about fifteen minutes later. He stopped his hired Jeep with a screech - God knew where he had managed to find a Jeep in rural Tuscany - and reversed back in a cloud of dust.

Leaving his door swinging and the Jeep in the middle of the road, he leapt down and pounced on the sacking parcel in the rear of the open Fiat.

"Can we help you?" asked Peter, mildly.

The American was red in the face and fit to explode.

"Where d'you get this?" he demanded.

"Up the road, young fellow at the monastery. He assured us it's the left arm of the Venus de Milo. Is something wrong with it?"

The American collected himself. He relinquished the marble arm in its sacking wrap. He shook his head in commiseration.

"I've been looking for the left arm of the Venus de Milo for over a year, but this isn't it. Sorry to have bothered you. I guess I got all excited over nothing."

"Oh, dear," said Angela, in anguish, "Do you mean we've been sold a pup?"

Shrugging, the American turned away to get back into his hired Jeep. Before he mounted to the driver's seat he seemed to have second thoughts.

"I don't like to see the little lady looking so sad," he said, "I'll take it off your hands for $50, how'll that be?"

Peter took out his pocket calculator.

"We paid in lira," he said, multiplying by a factor of two, "Let's see, today's dollar exchange rate, hmmm. Actually that was about $450."

"Done!" exclaimed the American, forgetting himself.

"But I don't want to sell it," complained Angela, "I like it."

"I'll give you another $100. That's a real good offer for a fake," said the American, "I'm doing you a real favour."

"Well, I don't know," agonised Peter, turning to Angela, "What do you think, darling?"

"What if it isn't a fake?" answered Angela in a stage whisper.

"It's kind of you," said Peter regretfully to the American, "but my wife........."

"Okay, okay!" The American was frantic. "I'll make it $600! Now, there's nobody going to give you better than that!"

"Goodness me! Do you have that kind of cash about you?" enquired Peter politely.

"Dollar traveller's cheques. Is that a problem?"

"No, no. Traveller's cheques will be fine. Peter and Angela Marks," Peter introduced themselves, holding out his hand, "I suppose we shake on the deal?"

The American shook his hand peremptorily, produced the cheque, filled it out, signed it, and passed it over. Peter passed it to Angela who slipped it quickly into her shoulder bag.

Cradling his prize, the American staggered with it a few steps. Peter helped him lift it into the back of the Jeep.

Peter and Angela drank a toast to him as he turned the jeep and drove away.

"And here's a toast to the enterprising young Eduardo," declared Peter, "I've never seem so many chunks of marble being turned into dismembered limbs, and probably heads, torsos, and complete bodies, too, as he had in that shed. A nice little family sideline. Along with the regular grave-stones and so on."

"He'd have to sell quite a few of them to buy that car," mused Angela, as they drove back to their hotel, "at his prices."

"Last year, right arms, this year left. There'll be another greedy American, or Englishman, or Dutchman, or whatever, along in a minute," Peter said.

As they drove through the town they passed a parked jeep. Two men stood at the rear looking at something inside wrapped in sacking. One was the American. The other was the man who had sat next to him on the plane and he was nodding eagerly as he produced his traveller's cheques and borrowed the American's pen.

Peter and Angela laughed.

"He is doubtless making a very nice fat profit," said Peter.

"We made some, too," mused Angela, "Do you think we should place some orders of our own?"

"No," said Peter, "that was a bit of fun, but we are *antiques* dealers."

Angela nodded. After a moment she said, "Do you realise we haven't been near an antique this holiday, if you don't count the wheel-barrow?"

"Quite right," said Peter, "Let's have a beer to celebrate."

They walked from the car to some pavement tables where the edges of the bright umbrellas were flapping gently in a freshening breeze.

They sat with two ice-cold beers, relaxed, and watched the world go by.

A man in a battered Panama hat was walking slowly along with dozens of helium-filled balloons, the strings grasped in one hand, the balloons floating like a bunch of strange giant silver grapes above his head. Each balloon was printed with the same cartoon face. A small child bought one and proudly carried the silver sphere bobbing past their table.

The breeze playfully flipped up the edge of the table-cloth and ruffled their hair.

The man with the balloons was having difficulty as the breeze grew stronger. Peter and Angela watched him trying to hold on his hat with one hand, the silver balloons bobbing and straining at their strings in the other.

One pulled free, and then another. Five or six balloons escaped, the grinning cartoon faces twisting this way as they flew high into the blue.

Peter and Angela watched them go, exchanged a smile, and raised their glasses to each other.

Each cartoon face was of a happy pig.

The Condition

In black tails, grey waistcoats, and discreetly striped silver cravats, Harry and Tom rose and turned towards the rear doors as the bridal music began.

Audrey, in a simple calf-length cream dress and a complicated beaded jacket, entered on the arm of an old family friend, her father having expired since her previous wedding some twenty-five years before. The organist was gamely attempting the tune by Scott Joplin she had specially requested instead of a conventional wedding march.

There was no irony intended. She had just loved the film with Paul Newman and Robert Redford. So Harry had lifted his shoulders in resignation and agreed to having the theme from *The Sting* played at his wedding. On one condition.

Audrey was not at all pleased with the condition. There was a little pre-nuptial silence over it.

As the days ticked by, Tom was forced to take action becoming diplomat, negotiator, referee, counsellor, and conciliator between his father and his prospective step-mother. There was no way Tom was going back to having his father around him, much as he loved him, cramping his lifestyle, because he was lonely and didn't know what to do with himself in the evenings. And weekends. And holidays.

Having persuaded his dad to take up dancing again, over-riding his moans that he'd forgotten how to dance and it wouldn't be the same without Tom's late mother, Tom was delighted when Harry met Audrey a few months later. Suddenly Harry was busy almost every night, practically every weekend, and planning holidays with Audrey instead of him. Long-widowed Audrey was just the spirited companion that his dad needed. The old man at fifty-two had plenty of life left in him yet.

The problem with his father was work. He took it very seriously. People expected Harry to be sober and grave when he attended on them. The sort of people who made up his clientele did not expect a frivolous man, a joker, a man who went dancing in his spare time. With clients he was always punctilious, correct. That was what they looked to him for. He had the appropriate words for the anxious client. The reassurances they needed. And if he gave them a time for delivery to their house he never, ever, failed to honour it.

When Audrey and Harry at last forgave each other, Tom breathed the greatest sigh of relief.

Audrey arrived at Harry's side as the last chord's of *The Entertainer* faded.

"You look wonderful, love," Harry said. Tom had been coaching him, taking no chances.

"Dearly beloved," began the vicar, and Tom checked again that the rings were still safe in his waistcoat pocket.

The congregation for this winter afternoon wedding was small. Just close friends and a few relatives.

A stifled sob indicated that Audrey's mother was enjoying the ceremony. Tom could just see her little feather hat. He was very glad to see her this once without her curlers and head-scarf. This was obviously the occasion she had been so long preparing for. Presumably she would go straight back into curlers afterwards to be ready for the next big special occasion. Perhaps one of Audrey's three sisters would oblige.

Tom wondered if he could slip something into his speech about it. It would either get him a laugh or get him crucified.

The photographer, visibly panicking about the poor light, posed everyone on the church steps and snapped rapidly through the set shots before they got too chilled.

The wedding guests hurried into the warmth of the cars that were taking them to the hotel where the champagne reception was to be held and Audrey turned to Harry.

"Now?" she asked in a resigned tone.

"Yes, love," said Harry, "Just as we agreed."

"I still can't believe you have to do this on our wedding day. What are people going to say?"

"If we don't get it up to the house today, Tom and I risk our good reputation. We'll be as quick as we decently can, Audrey love."

Audrey pouted, which looked more appealing than it should on a woman of forty-nine, and accepted a kiss.

"Right, step on it, son," said Harry, as they got into Tom's car for the two-mile drive to their workshop, "Have you put everything into the other car?"

"Yes, Dad. Relax. Everything's ready to go."

At the workshop they transferred rapidly to the specially adapted estate they used for their business.

Harry put on his seatbelt, switched on his headlights, checked over his shoulder that the long mahogany shape in the back was properly secure, and drew smoothly away. Ten minutes later he was braking gently to a standstill in a neat close of detached houses.

Tom rang the bell of Number 15, noticing as he waited that a 'Sold' sign was lying in the grass by the drive of Number 16 and a young woman inside, silhouetted against the light, was putting up curtains.

The new neighbour paused in her curtain hanging. She could see someone was at the door of Number 15. She saw the door open and illuminated in the warm light spilling out the figure of a man in a tail-coat. He turned and went to the rear of a large dark estate vehicle where he and another man, also in tails, slid out a long wooden box from the back. One at each end, they carried it reverently between them into the house. They returned after a minute, collected a smaller box, and what was possibly a tool bag, and closed the tail-gate of the vehicle. The door of Number 15 shut behind them.

"Good heavens," said the young woman to her husband, who was bringing in mugs of tea, "I think someone's died next door!"

"Very strange," he said, frowning, "They're not young, but I saw them bringing in their shopping earlier. Seemed all right then."

He peered out at the dark car just as the street lights came on.

They drank their tea in thoughtful silence.

"Are coffins made to measure?" she finally asked.

"Um, I don't really know."

"You saw the people at Number 15, is one of them very thin?"

"Thin?"

"And very tall?" She stared out of the window again. "Oh, look, the men have come out again. They're *running* to their car!"

"*Running?*" said her husband, "Not what you expect, is it?"

Harry reversed, swung the wheel, and accelerated out of the close.

"I though they'd never stop talking!" he said in anguish, "Poor Audrey. Oh, god, she'll kill me."

"Give her mum the chance to take her curlers out again," said Tom.

"What?"

"Nothing. Just drive. I'll sit here and worry about my speech."

The new occupants of Number 16 looked at each other.

"We should go round," said the wife.

"Perhaps you're right," said her husband, "Best put on a coat, then."

"Straight to the reception!" declared Harry, "You can get your car tomorrow."

"Fine by me," said Tom. "You're the one who worries that this thing looks like a hearse."

"I don't care any more. Well, I'll park in a dark corner. Put the radio on."

Tom switched on the car radio just in time for the news. The weather report followed. Snow was expected on high ground and already falling in most parts of Scotland.

Harry shot his son a wide pleased grin.

"Excellent!" he said, zipping across at a traffic light just before it went to red and into the hotel car-park.

"We're here. Let's get inside and take what coming to us."

Audrey looked quite happy to see them.

Linking her arm into Harry's, she walked with him up the grand staircase to the room hired for the reception.

"I'm sorry I was so long, love," said Harry, "They would keep on talking."

"We watched *Four Weddings and a Funeral* on the lounge video. I hardly missed you at all. Were they pleased with it?"

"Oh, yes. They say they'll recommend us to everyone they know."

"So you still have a business to keep a roof over our heads and for Tom to inherit. She smiled over her shoulder at Tom who was coming up the stairs behind them. "Well, that's good."

"Oh, yes," said Harry, suddenly remembering, "And it's snowing in Scotland."

"That's marvellous!"

The door of Number 15 was opened by a comfortable lady in comfortable velvet trousers and a comfortable knitted top. On her doorstep she found a young couple dressed alike in jeans, sweatshirts and waxed green jackets. They looked very anxious.

"Hello," she said tentatively.

The young woman spoke.

"We've just moved into Number 16," she said.

"Oh, that's nice. You've come to introduce yourselves. I'm Jean. Do come in."

"We noticed the men in tail-coats ......," ventured the young woman.

Jean laughed.

"Looking for all the world like a couple of undertakers! Come through to the kitchen, it's cosier. That, staring enraptured at his clock, is my husband. it's just been repaired. Paul! Say hello to our new neighbours."

Behind Jean, the young woman shared a look with her own husband, eyes very wide, a hand to her open mouth.

"A *clock!*" she whispered, "It was a *long-case clock!*"

Unbidden, a giggle rose up.

Jean had very good hearing.

"My dear," she said, highly entertained, "You didn't think ....? no wonder you both looked so worried! Hear that, Paul? The young lady though it was a coffin being carried in. A long-case coffin. How lovely! It'd be just what he'd want. too. I'll have to make sure he gets one!"

Tom paused for the laughter and applause. Audrey and her sisters rocked with laughter at the reference to their mother's curlers. He raised his glass.

"A toast to the Bride and Groom!"

The guests echoed him, lifting their glasses.

"The Bride and Groom!"

Tom saw his father and his father's new wife exchange a lingering glance.

Thank goodness for that, he thought and relaxed. He looked around at the happy guests. He was looking for the rather attractive girl he had seen earlier wearing a fake-fur hat.

The following morning Tom firmly interrupted Harry's last-minute instructions.

"Dad! The hired clothes will go back on Monday. Before ten. The moon-roller clock in the workshop will be ready to deliver when you get back. Yes, my mate Phil *will* be helping me. We won't drop it. It will work perfectly. The owners will be very happy and recommend us to all their friends. You will still have a business to come back to! So, have a great time. Don't break anything on the slopes."

He kissed his new step-mother, gave his father a hug and bundled them both into the estate car. With brightly coloured skis stacked in the back instead of the long case of a clock, it no longer resembled a hearse.

"Now, just go!"

Tom waved them away.

Taking a torn piece of paper napkin from his pocket, he went inside. He read the number that had been hastily scrawled there with an eyebrow pencil, lifted the telephone, and dialled it.

Black Diamond

Dora pushed between a fat lady with a basket and a stocky porter but the crowd around the man who had just stepped off the London train proved impenetrable.

They had pressed up from all over the station to hear the details.

"What time was this?" asked the station-master, a turnip watch, regulation issue, at this moment in his hand as though preparing to make some calculation.

As the news the traveller brought rippled outwards to her edge of the throng, Dora made a long arm and managed to tug the greatcoat of a man further in.

"Come on, Joe!" she said.

The crowd were avid for more. The man from London felt rather overwhelmed by his sudden position as spokesman for Royalty. He began to repeat his story. But the Railways had a time-table to keep. Slamming doors, the guard's whistle, and the heavy grunting of the steam-engine pulling out of the station drowned his words.

"Joe!"

Joe eased himself out of the crush.

"Us'd better tell the maister," he said.

"That we will," said Dora, impatiently mounting the cart, shrugging off Joe's assistance, "And as quickly as possible!"

She tucked the coarse travelling rug round her knees. Joe, clicking his tongue to the horse, his breath vaporising on the December air, took them clattering out of the station yard.

Glancing back, Dora saw the ticket collector giving directions to the man from London amid the dispersing crowd. People spilled out across the cobbles, some sadly quiet, others eager to spread the news to any acquaintance they met.

"Fast as you can, Joe," said Dora. In those remaining moments before the rest of Whitby, indeed the whole country, knew what she knew, she was experiencing not sorrow, but hope.

Her father was in the workshop. While his handful of employees toiled at the benches and polishing machines, he pored over his ledgers as though they could tell him a different story from the one he already knew.

He saw Dora jump down from the cart and come running in. The sight of her expression, the brightness of her eyes, filled him with deep misgivings.

"Dear God, lass! Tha's not come to tell me tha's met some fine lad and want to get wed, has tha'?"

Dora was stopped short by this outrageous parental assumption.

"Only think on," said her father, warningly, "Unless he's a rich bugger and loves thee for tha' goodness alone, thou'll have to tell him it's not on. I can't run to a fancy do right now. All we've got will have to go towards a cheap funeral, for I'm thinking of slipping from this world before our creditors get their hands on the business."

"Father!" exclaimed Dora, reprovingly, "No more of this 'Better-off-Without-Me' nonsense. Please! "

"Well," sulked the old man, "Coming in like it were tha' birthday and Christmas rolled together.......... What is it then?"

"A man from London........." began Dora.

"What!" roared her father, "I'll not have my only child marrying some gert soft Southerner! That's final! Is he rich?"

He became aware that his workforce could hear him above the noise of the machines and had paused to listen.

"What am I paying tha' for?" he bellowed and they bent over their tasks again.

"Father!" shouted Dora, exasperated, "I'm not thinking of getting wed! The man from London brought some news which might do us a bit of good!"

"There's no man wanting to wed thee?

"No."

Greatly cheered, Dora's father magnanimously prepared to listen.

"We won't have a lot of time if we're to act on this," said Dora.

Following the line of the ticket collector's arm, Robert Lucas saw first a cart leaving the station yard at a fine clip, second the face of the young woman on the cart looking back over her shoulder, and then the road he was being directed to take.

Walking briskly, for it was very cold, he reflected that he had not been in this part of the country since he was a baby and his family moved South with his father's search for work.

News - his news - had gone ahead of him and black stuff was being draped at the portal of the inn when he reached it. He was welcomed gravely.

"How long will tha' be staying, sir?" asked the landlord, deferentially.

"Two or three nights - my business here should take no longer than that."

"What line of business would that be, sir?" the landlord asked conversationally as he led the way upstairs.

Robert Lucas, inspecting the accommodation, appeared not to hear the question. As secretary to a private gentleman, it was not his place to tell the landlord of an inn what he was engaged on. The renting of a summer residence for his employer was regarded a confidential matter.

"This will be fine," he said, adding, "Sad news from London."

"It is that, sir," the landlord agreed, "Round here, mind, such news might be received with a bit less weeping and wailing than perhaps some other places."

"Why is that?" asked Robert Lucas.

"On account of business. It's fish, mostly. And shellfish. Thou'll have noticed that on the air, no doubt ...."

Just then a boy of about twelve interrupted from the doorway.

"Ma says: will the gentleman take his dinner now?"

"Yes, thank you, I'll be down as soon as I've washed," said Robert Lucas, turning to the washstand.

The landlord and his son withdrew.

"It'll be quite proper," Dora assured her father, "It's only business, after all. Joe will drive me."

"I should go," protested her father, but he had given in. He would give orders to the workers, Dora would do what else was needed

He had taken from the storeroom a six foot long black lump about six inches wide. He fondly reminisced as they gazed on it.

"The largest piece ever dug out, that. Black diamond. The man I bought it from told me he offered it to the British Museum as a curiosity for 10 guineas. I offered him the same to take it off his hands. He was sharper than he looked. I had to pay fifteen pound in the end." He chuckled. "It were a bargain, anyroad." His mood changed to gloom again. "But folk follows fashion. There's been little call for it lately. I should have put my money in a fishing boat. Folk's always have to eat."

"Right," said Dora briskly, cutting him short, "We'll get on then."

She went first to the railway station, where she spoke to the ticket collector, and then to the inn where Robert Lucas was staying.

"He's at his dinner," said the landlady to Dora's request, "I'll send the boy to ask. Jack! See if Mr. Lucas'll have his meal disturbed to see a young lady what's come."

Dora waited, musing on the landlady's sweetness of temperament.

"Says he'll see her," young Jack reported. He was already learning to be as pleasant as his Ma. "Says to bring another cup and saucer and could he have some mustard."

Robert rose as Dora came in. He knew her face immediately.

"You go on eating," she said, "and I'll tell you why I'm here. You will no doubt know what the main business of Whitby is."

"Fishing, I'm told," replied Robert, "But I have no interest in it other than that I sometimes eat fish."

Dora stared for a moment and then she laughed. Robert smiled, uncertain how his remark had been funny.

The landlady bore in a cup and saucer and a small dish of mustard which she clattered down on a table by the door, leaving again without a word.

Robert and Dora exchanged a glance, his expression wryly amazed, hers merry.

"I'll fetch them," she said, "I'd better explain myself. Your main use to me is that you come from London and you'll have contacts there. My father has a business here in Whitby, but apart from holiday visitors we've not much commerce with London folk. Our little business has kept food on our table and paid our few workers but little else. Like my father says, folk will always need to eat and dress themselves but they don't need adornments. If we're to improve, I shall have to push a bit. Would you tell me how long you'll be here?"

"Just a few days."

"Good," said Dora, "I won't be the only one to approach you while you're here. So the less time for you to have any other offer made you, the better for my father and me. We want an agent to sell our goods in London. We have the materials to meet any demand. We will provide you with a range of samples. You take the orders and send them to me, my father fulfils them, I despatch them, and we pay you a percentage. There is going to be a great demand and we are ready for it. You're looking blank, Mr. Lucas. Did no-one ever tell you what Whitby is famous for?"

She indicated the neck of her buttoned jacket.

"This, Mr. Lucas."

He saw a large carved black brooch.

"I'm afraid I don't know much about women's jewellery," he said, apologetically.

Dora took from a small bag an ornately carved cross.

"This then. Regard the workmanship closely. These items are made from jet, Mr. Lucas. It is the only suitable material for mourning items."

Robert turned the cross over and over in his hands, glanced shyly at the brooch Dora wore.

"But I have a position already," he said at last.

"Will it make you rich?"

"I shouldn't think so. Tomorrow, when I've begun on my employer's business, I'll have some time. Perhaps we can talk again?"

Dora considering whether to say more, saw the landlady coming in.

"There's someone asking for you," said the landlady.

Dora held out her hand to Robert.

"Make me one promise," she said, "See no-one on this subject until we speak again. After that you must do as you please."

Robert shook Dora's hand and she left.

"I'll see no-one tonight," he told the landlady.

She sniffed and went to give the caller his message.

"That's it, Dora," said her father at breakfast, throwing down The Times, "The papers have it! We've lost our advantage."

"No we haven't. He's at the door now."

Robert was shown in by their maid-of-all-work. He stood looking somewhat dazed in their breakfast room.

"Will you take coffee, Mr. Lucas?" asked Dora, sweetly.

"I came to view the property for my employer," said Robert.

"I know. We rent it out every summer," she said, "We have a little cottage we live in then."

"That's her idea," grunted Dora's father, "Has tha' seen the paper? Prince Albert's dead and the Queen, the Court, and the whole country will be going into mourning. What does tha' think on that?"

Robert stood thinking in the middle of the pleasant room. He looked across at Dora who proffered him a brimming coffee cup. The aroma was most enticing. He turned back to her father and met a face of thunder.

"Has tha' got thoughts on marrying my daughter, young man?"

Robert accepted the cup of coffee. Dora smiled at him.

"I do believe I have, sir," he said, taking a sip.

"Well tha' had better be rich, then!"

Robert smiled at Dora.

"I think I will be," he said.

Wings of Fortune

Somewhere at the far end of the cavernous shed someone was cheerfully whistling. It was a working whistle, accompanied by the whine and buzz of electric tools, and underpinned by intermittent hammering.

As far as the eye could see huge tables, vast chiffoniers, break-front bookcases, sets of chairs, and enormous kitchen dressers stood on the flagged floor, those furthest away looking quite normal sized until you reached them.

An inner sanctum of plywood panels enclosed the machinery and manpower of the workshop where repair and restoration was taking place and which was the source of the blithe whistling.

No-one was immediately visible, but Annabel Shore, who had paused in the doorway to take it all in, freshly amazed by the scale of the objects and their setting, made her way confidently between the items of furniture feeling like Alice in Wonderland during her reduced phase.

She glanced at the few vases and dishes displayed on the giant furniture as she passed, automatically assessing them, but it was near the plywood partitioning that she found what she had come for.

A dozen tatty cardboard boxes, jammed untidily to overflowing with the detritus of someone's life, lay on the flags. The brothers, Darren and Tyrone, had done another house clearance.

The boxes contained the items they had no use for in their business. Items that were too small for them to take an interest in. Annabel knew there would be stuff in the boxes that she would have no interest in either, but there might be treasure too. She had bought from the brothers before and turned a useful profit.

As she began to look through the largest box, sounds beyond the partition ceased. There was a scraping noise, and a wide section of panelling was folded back. Two large men carried out a mahogany table with legs like a rugby player - except for the fluting - that could have seated twenty close acquaintances or ten people who were not on speaking terms.

"Hello, love," said the slighter of the two, probably a mere 16-stones compared to his brother's 18, "Be with you in a tick. Over by the moggy chairs, Daz. They might all go as a set."

They placed the table down by the serried ranks of a small army of mahogany dining chairs near the wall, plonked a candelabra in the centre, and strolled back.

"You having this lot, then?" asked Tyrone, in casual but not unfriendly tones, "It's sixty-five to you. All modern, but some people like that."

Annabel shoved back the items she had pulled out in order to investigate deeper. Anything after the death of the last George was modern to Tyrone, but this lot did seem to be mostly twentieth century.

"I'll get a brew on, shall I, Ty?" asked Darren. He knew which of them ran the outfit.

"Good idea, Daz," said Tyrone, "And then you can give the young lady a hand out with these if she wants them, okay?"

"I'll just plug in the kettle."

Annabel would have liked to have been selective in which boxes she wanted to take. The greasy smell and the handles poking out of some of the smaller boxes suggested they contained kitchenalia of the most unsaleable kind. But the system did not work that way. You bought the lot or none at all. No picking and choosing.

After a house clearance, when the nice furniture had been put to one side for a quick polish and ready profit, the nice-but-in-need-of-attention furniture was put to another side for a spell in the workshop. The "other" furniture was sent along to the local auction to get shot of it, and all that was left was the stuff in boxes. There were always things in them that absolutely no one wanted, but that was not the brothers' problem. That was the problem of whoever bought the boxes.

"I'll take them," said Annabel, decisively.

She had delved far enough to know she could at least cover her sixty-five pounds and make some profit. There might be more profit at the bottom. Or there might not. There would certainly be things for donation to one of the many Charity Shops she supported from time to time, and, finally, things fit only to be taken to the local Council Recycling Depot, formerly known as The Dump.

She handed over the cash.

She began in her back yard. One of the other tenants of the converted house, in which she had a small ground floor flat, paused to watch with amusement, and some horror, as Annabel pulled on rubber gloves and began to unpack her purchases.

"From this she makes a living?" he asked the air beside him.

"Yes, I know, Paul," sighed Annabel, "If I had any sense, with my history degree and a nice smile, I could be dishing up hamburgers and fries for £1.50 an hour."

"Have you found anything to make your fortune in there?"

"Not my fortune. Not yet. Come back later."

Paul left her to it.

Returning a few hours later, he found Annabel crouched over a bucket of soapy water, removing the last few items and drying them on an old towel. At one side of the yard, tellingly close to the dustbins, were several boxes repacked for disposal. She was singing softly as she worked. It was a happy, contented sound.

"A fortune?" he asked.

"We-ell," she replied, cautiously, "I need a strong light, a good magnifying glass, a copy of Godden's, and a couple of Collectables price guides before I can tell you. They were rather mixed boxes, and the household they came from must have been more than a little eccentric! Give me a hand indoors with these and I'll show you."

"Are they disinfected?" asked her neighbour, warily.

"Totally. Some things need a bit of polish, but we can bring them into the building without fear or special clothing."

Annabel, laying out items on her pine kitchen table, explained.

"Okay, these are the obvious things worth having," she said "One chrome table lamp - in need of polishing up, not to mention re-wiring, but with glass shade intact. Some silver plated items - also in need of polish. One undamaged Clarice Cliffe plate - my stake-money back in itself! Some cups, saucers, bowls, jugs, and plates to be checked out further with Mr. Godden's invaluable guide to makers' marks. Some bits of pressed glass. A carved breadboard with bread knife. This looks like a wedding present that was never actually used. Some Bakelite bits - string holder, couple of ashtrays. A teapot shaped like a tank. Unfortunately the spout is chipped, but possibly restorable. A biscuit tin full of buttons and sewing items. A handful of costume jewellery."

"None of that seems particularly eccentric to me," remarked Paul, idly picking up and examining the items, "Except perhaps this teapot shaped like a tank."

"None of that is eccentric," said Annabel, lifting a box from under the table, "This, however, is one I prepared earlier. Item: a flight of Mallard duck wall decorations by Beswick, in excellent condition under the layer of grime I had to clean off. Item: a flight of seagulls circa 1930. Item: a kingfisher. And the rest. There are twelve different ornithological specimens altogether. And this. This is the proof of eccentricity."

She handed Paul some crumpled photographs of various parts of a very dull 1930's semi, each showing a display of china wall birds in flight.

Annabel leaned over to point out the finer details.

"You see? Every wall. Over the bed, in the loo, both walls of the hall, up the stairs. Over the fireplace, of course. In the kitchen, naturally. But it was some time ago, I think, because grimy as they were, they had obviously been packed away long before the brothers came to clear the place. Luckily they didn't bother to do more than rip off a bit of the newspaper from the top few items. Not their sort of thing anyway. But they might have asked a lot more if they had checked further down."

Paul came to the last photograph.

"Oh, my!" he said.

Annabel smiled.

"They did seem to have a thing about flights of birds, didn't they?"

They looked at the picture together. Seated in a row on a sofa, with a flight of pottery Guinness toucans clearly visible on the wall behind, were three live toucans of gradually diminishing size. Each with glasses of Guinness seemingly balanced on a bright orange bill. A Daddy toucan, a Mummy toucan, and a Baby toucan about ten years old.

"They must have been going to a party," said Paul.

"One would hope so," said Annabel, "We'll give them the benefit of the doubt. We'll try hard to believe they didn't dress like that every night in the privacy of their own home, but it won't be easy."

"So," said Paul, "Are these Mallards and Toucans and the other winged things worth anything?"

"Oh, yes," said Annabel, happily, "I have to put them in front of the right buyers, but I'm unlikely to get this lucky with the brothers' boxes again."

"In that case, can I invite you out for Chinese Crispy Duck to celebrate?"

"Yes. Thanks. That would be great. But first I need a bath in Dettol or neat bleach or something. Where there's brass, there's a lot of muck. Do I need to dress up?"

Paul looked at the photograph still in his hand and back to Annabel.

"Ah, no," he said quietly, "Informal dress will be fine."

A little later, as the waiter shredded their Crispy Duck in a blur of flying forks, Paul raised his glass.

"Here's to your wings of fortune!" he said.

"Better than hamburger and fries!" re-joined Annabel, "This time."

Bloodstones

"**W**ear them?" Isaac Morris exclaimed, "Diamonds like that are not for wearing, they are for stealing and fencing!"

"I promised her," said John Miller. He was a broad man, enriched with good living, his hair just developing neat wings of silver. He stood squarely in the small space between the door and the counter, almost filling it.

Isaac bustled about his tiny emporium agitatedly, almost superstitiously, checking the locks on his display cabinets and the grilles on his window and door.

"Let her wear the paste," he said, "What will she know? Leave them where they are safe. Such colour, such fire in their hearts! In a trice they would be gone from her neck! From her ears! They will not care, the thieves, if they hurt her pretty ears. There has been more blood than a couple of torn ears over these stones. "

"The stories are exaggerated," said John Miller, reasonably. "And if there was ever any truth in them at all, it was all long ago." He had an easy smile. "You worry too much, Isaac."

"I worry? It is called security-consciousness, this worrying of mine!"

"I've arranged insurance ...."

Isaac snorted and twirled a hand in the air. A long-fingered hand, thin and freckled with age.

"Insurance is just money! They pay you to replace what is stolen with the equivalent - what could be equivalent to those diamonds? We have trust between us, John Miller. Even a bank could not give you such security as I give you. Too many people would know your business."

"Isaac, listen. For twenty-four hours I want to give Zara the pleasure of wearing the diamonds instead of the paste. She has barely seen them. Just for her birthday, is it too much for a man to give his lovely wife what she asks?"

Isaac sighed, spreading his arms.

"What you talk of here is love. In the face of it, I melt. Your lovely Zara shall have the diamonds. But we make proper arrangements. You are not walking out with them casually in your pocket like small change. I will send my son with them to your house – putting his very life in danger! – and you will sign a proper receipt. Tomorrow, he will bring them back."

John Miller smiled at the old man.

"Isaac," he said, "I will see your son at my house at six o' clock. Goodbye!"

Isaac unlocked the door, saw John Miller out, re-locked it behind him and set the alarms.

John Miller closed the glass partition between himself and his driver and opened his laptop. He connected to the internet via his car-phone and profitably moved some of his shares whilst he was driven to Bond Street where he had an appointment. Some small antique silver items had been reserved for his consideration and he was hoping to find something exquisite to add to his already extensive personal collection. An hour later, he returned to his car with a new treasure, made bookings for the evening, and rang his wife.

Zara Miller was talking on her mobile phone, pacing the first-floor sitting room, when the trilling of the telephone on the coffee table interrupted her.

"Just a moment, Kit," she said and, putting down the mobile, answered the other phone.

She listened to her husband telling her about the theatre seats he had booked and the restaurant he would be taking her to.

"And the diamonds?" she asked, and heard him laugh.

"It's all arranged – you shall wear the diamonds,"

"Oh, thank you darling! I'm so excited!"

"I'll be home about five." John Miller rang off.

Replacing the telephone handset on its rest, Zara took up her mobile phone again.

By six o'clock the Millers had prepared themselves for the evening.

In typical fashion John Miller had changed his mind about the theatre and booked for an opera instead.

Zara, who would have preferred the cinema, decided it didn't matter. She smiled up at him as she finished tying his bow tie, feeling the diamonds heavy at her neck and ears.

She had seen them only once before, in Isaac Morris's tiny shop, shortly before she and John were married. She had been shown the three large flawless stones, each surrounded by seven smaller stones, set in 24-carat red gold as a pair of earrings and a pendant on a long chain and been told they were mined in Russia in the eighteenth century.

Looking at the amazing cold flame that burned deep inside each stone, with Isaac Morris hovering protectively, she had asked about their bad reputation.

Even before the diamonds were cut and set, she heard, the owner of the mine where they were found contracted the plague, carried the infection into his family's home, and suffered the loss of his wife and every one of their five children before he himself died.

The Dutchman who cut the stones was reputed to have fainted when he struck the first blow on the largest of them because he was so nervous – but that had been told of other diamonds.

A Russian nobleman had the cut stones set for his wife. She unfortunately died in childbirth and her distraught husband, blaming the stones for bringing bad luck, gave them away to a rather poorer, less emotional, cousin.

The diamonds were lost for a while but turned up again in Holland. The rich merchant who acquired them was killed by a runaway cart in Rotterdam a few weeks later. The daughter who inherited them sailed to America and died soon after from blood poisoning. Her teenage son and heir was struck dumb and put into an institution and the diamonds disappeared again.

They were found by a coroner's officer in New York in the filthy rags of an unidentified vagrant found dead in an alley one Christmas Eve in the nineteen-fifties. They were put into a museum and stolen a month later. Two security guards were killed in the raid.

Decades later, the diamonds were anonymously, but very publicly, donated to a politician in Virginia by throwing them through his office window in a metal box with a note attached. The politician offered to return them to the museum they had been stolen from but the museum declined them in favour of a donation to buy a painting instead. So the diamonds were auctioned and were bought by the very wealthy John Miller.

"How do we know they are the same ones that were blamed for all that plague and dying?" asked Zara.

"There are mine accounts, stone-cutter's records, the goldsmith's drawings, letters, wills, inventories, coroner's records, and photographs. We know from scratched marks on the gold mounts that they certainly spent some time in a pawnbroker's shop. Their provenance has been thoroughly researched," said John, "And I'm not superstitious."

Zara had stared long at the diamonds, saw them flash like strobe lights in a clear pool before John closed the box on their glory. They brought away with them a paste copy that would fool anyone but a true expert while the real thing remained in the guardianship of old Isaac Morris.

Zara yawned during the opera. John did not see. He really enjoyed opera. He assumed she did, too. She checked her watch. She closed her hand about the heavy pendant at her breast and smiled to herself.

In a way it was disappointing to be wearing the diamonds, the notorious diamonds, and have no-one notice. No one walks about in million-pound diamonds these days. Most people seeing them would think them merely good costume jewellery.

At last the audience were applauding. They cheered and called.

God, thought Zara, they want the fat man on the stage to do an encore! She checked her watch again. Kit would just have to wait.

As John and Zara were being shown to their table at the restaurant, a dark-haired man rose from a table near the door and went out. Zara excused herself and headed for the Ladies Rest Room. The dark-haired man was by the telephone in the hall. She glanced at his face as she passed,

In the rest-room cubicle Zara removed the diamonds and laid them in a man's handkerchief. From her handbag she took the paste copies. Her hands were shaking. She took a few moments to compose herself.

In the hall, the man was still by the telephone.

"Would you have change for a pound coin?" he asked, a little loudly. Dropping his voice, he hissed fiercely, "Why are you so late? I don't know how many coffees I've had to drink, waiting!"

"Sorry, Kit, there were three encores," Zara muttered, taking some items out of her bag in a hunt for her purse and laying them by the telephone. "*And* he nearly changed his mind about *this* restaurant."

A waiter coming past smiled politely but took no other notice.

Kit stared at Zara's ears and throat.

"How do you know they're the right ones?"

"The real ones have scratched marks at the back. I'd have to show you," said Zara, softly. Louder, she said, "Here we are, a fifty, two twenty pences and a 10p. Does that help you?"

She scooped everything back into her bag except the man's handkerchief. Kit casually pocketed it. It was done. Another passing waiter stood aside to let Zara by as she hurried back to the dining room.

She smiled at her husband as she sat down.

"I've ordered for you," said John, "You were ages."

"Sorry, darling," she said, "Someone wanted change for the telephone."

The sommelier appeared and poured their champagne.

John raised his glass.

"To my beautiful wife. Happy Birthday, darling. You look radiant. Perhaps we should get the real stones out more often."

Zara smiled. Their first course arrived, beautifully presented, but she had little appetite.

Their dessert dishes had been cleared, Zara's barely touched, and they were sipping brandy when John's driver brought him an urgent message.

"A break-in at the house?" John exclaimed, annoyed by both the interruption of his evening and the assault on his property. "Have the police been called? Get us back there – now!"

Butterflies were dancing in Zara's stomach. The second part was over. It was unfortunate, but it was done.

The place was a mess. Kit had left the large television, two VCRs and a computer stacked just inside the ground floor window he had got in by.

"They knew what they were doing," commented one of the police officers, "The alarms have been disabled, but it looks like they were disturbed before they could have that lot away." It did.

Some of Zara's jewellery, which was assumed to include the copy diamonds, had been taken, but little else was missing. John's collection of small silver that had taken him years to accumulate was untouched.

"Not connoisseurs of antiques, then," added the officer, "We'll have the place dusted for fingerprints, but every petty thief knows to wear gloves these days. If you could make out a list of the jewellery and anything else that's missing, sir, it would be helpful and your insurance company will need it. Tomorrow will do. It's lucky the lady's wearing the really good stuff."

"Yes," agreed John, tiredly, "Yes, it is."

John Miller rang the bell of Isaac Morris's premises first thing in the morning expecting strong reproof for carrying the diamonds through the street in his pocket, even though he had come in his car with the doors locked and his driver as bodyguard.

Isaac locked the door as soon as he had admitted him. He opened the box and fitted an eyeglass to examine the contents.

"They're quite safe," John said, "They were never out of my sight. There isn't a scratch on them."

Isaac took the glass from his eye and looked up at him.

"You are wrong, John Miller," he said, "There is. But that is just as it should be."

Zara Miller paced, talking on her mobile phone.

"I won't be coming. I decided last night that I don't like you as much as I like John. I thought I did, but it was a mistake. Don't bother looking for the scratches I mentioned. You won't find them. Goodbye, Kit."

A Few Bob at the Door

Iris Jackson, rocking her youngest in the pram, stood by her gate to see her three eldest off to school.

For a moment the children were lost to sight as a horse and cart with a motor car right behind it came down the narrow lane. The sleek motor car parped its horn imperiously. The carter inclined his head in greeting to Iris as he drew level, conspiratorially tossing his head back over his shoulder and rolling his eyes to heaven. His horse snorted at the sudden blare but went on planting down great fringed hooves with not the slightest change of pace.

Then the children were visible again, waving to Iris one by one from the stile as they clambered over to cross the fields. With a sharp clap and whirr of wings wood-pigeons flew up from the newly-ploughed furrows at the children's approach.

Iris saw the pigeons, a cloud of flapping dots silvered above by the early sunlight, dark below, turning together to flow across the open sky for the safety of the trees.

The greedy beggars would be back among the furrows before the children reached the far gate, Iris thought. The baby was quiet now. Iris went indoors to get her morning washing out on the line.

A little further down the lane a man stepping aside to let the cart and motor car pass also gazed after the children and looked up at the pigeons winging across the washed blue sky. He smiled on the pretty rural idyll.

"Blimey," he said softly to himself, strolling up the lane as if he had all the time in the world, "There's even roses round the ruddy door."

He peered in at the sleeping baby as he knocked at the cottage door.

When Iris appeared, frowning, drying reddened hands on her apron, a toddler behind her sucking her thumb on the narrow stairs, he raised his hat.

"Anything to sell? Any bits and bobs, trinkets and the like, what would do you better in ready cash? Lovely family, missus. Must be a worry, all them new shoes. Any sticks of furniture taking up too much room? Any rings and things, china and brass? You must have something I could give you a few bob for. You have a look. No hurry. I'll wait right here."

Iris looked the man over. Not a new suit, but well-pressed. Sturdy boots that had walked quite a few miles. Celluloid collar to save on washing. The politely raised hat just losing its shape. A Londoner by his voice. Iris had been to London once with her husband and rather enjoyed the bustle and the shops.

It was true she could use a few bob. She had seen some nice material last market day that she could run up for the girls and herself. Her eldest boy needed new trousers. And shoes. Shoes for the biggest girl, too.

She pondered on just what she had to sell. All her furniture was hand-me-down. Heavy, old-fashioned stuff that no-one would want these days.

She had her mother's locket that she never wore and her mother's rings, all very old-fashioned. She slipped them into her apron pocket.

Iris stared at the mantelpiece over the range. Two silly dogs with flat backs.

The best oil-lamp. A fancy, fiddly, little chiming clock and a Chinese crock with a lid which they used for putting cash and keys and lost buttons in.

The china dogs were a keepsake from Tom's mother's house when she died, so Iris could not get rid of those. When they finally got the long-promised electricity to the cottage, Iris was going to bury that ugly, messy, old lamp at the end of the garden with the rubbish. The old chiming clock, also from Tom's mother's house, was better at keeping letters and bills from slipping off the shelf than keeping time, but Tom liked the thing.

Iris opened the cupboard beside the fireplace. Apart from their everyday crockery, none of it matching, the round biscuit tin with her sewing things and the flat biscuit tin in which she kept their insurance policies, there were the things that were in here because they belonged nowhere. A linen table-cloth tied with lilac ribbon, too good to use. A box of old Christmas cards and postcards. A cardboard box of inherited medals from the Boer War and the Great War.

Fleetingly, Iris wondered if there would be another war as some people were saying. Perhaps Tom, now thirty, would be too old to go. It was hard enough living on a farm labourer's wage, if he went for a soldier she didn't know how she would manage.

There were the vases Tom had never liked. They had been in that cupboard since they moved into the cottage. Someone had given them the pair of vases as a wedding present. Tom was insulted because they hadn't been bought new, just taken out of someone's house and wrapped up to do.

Iris lifted them down from the top shelf. Tom wouldn't mind about these.

The man was whistling softly, hands in pockets, leaning his shoulder against the door-frame. He took one of the vases from Iris, tapped it, up-ended it and pulled a face before standing it down on the doorstep.

He took the second one, tapping it and running his finger around the rim and the base almost idly, without looking at what he was doing.

"What else have you got? Rings and things? Ah. Very pretty, but...."

He put down the second vase and took out an eyeglass to examine the locket and the rings. Iris watched closely.

"Well, now," he said, smiling, "What's a pair of shoes for a growing boy, or a pretty girl or two? What's your husband earn? Not enough, eh? Never quite enough, is it? Tell you what. It's a lovely day. I'll give you a fiver for the lot. That's a good week's wages for anybody. You can tell your husband what a clever girl you've been."

He unfolded a five pound note and held it up for Iris to see. Then he folded it and put it in her hand, closing her fingers over it and smiling. This close, she could smell his bad breath.

Iris decided she didn't like his oily manner. She didn't like his yellow smile. With the money in her apron pocket, she couldn't wait to see him go. It was market day and she hadn't got all her washing on the line yet, the baby would be waking up, and she still had to walk into the town.

The gold locket and rings in his pocket, the vases in an old shopping bag, the man raised his hat at the gate before strolling on up the lane. His mate was not far away with the motor-van. He grinned. He told him there was good stuff to be had in these cottages.

Market day anywhere brings a place to life.

Vegetable sellers bawled their wares, shovelling potatoes and onions into open shopping bags. Pans hanging like bunting jangled gently in the breeze. Fish stank the air. Flowers in galvanised buckets sweetened it again. Fabric unravelled in yards from stacked rolls, brightly coloured and sober, rough-measured straight across from the seller's left shoulder to his outstretched right hand. Ribbons and buttons and threads. Toffee broken up by hammer and tipped from trays into little paper cones. Gipsies appearing from nowhere. Women with shopping baskets nervously paying over coins for sprigs of heather and lucky charms. Some Romany still sold clothes' pegs and sharpened knives, but they were very few now.

While older people moaned about changes, Iris loved them.

Motorbikes and sidecars, glossy cars, movie stars, and new things in shops like Cushings, the big store in the high street. Not as big as some of the shops she had seen in London, but it was pretty grand for a small country town and Iris could gaze on clothes she could never afford, items for the home that she would never have, electrical goods she could not use, china in the latest designs, bed linen, children's toys, and furniture. She wondered who had such smart furniture in their homes. Perhaps those who lived in the new villa houses on the outskirts.

She could see who wore the fashions. Bright young things who lived in the grander houses and came to town in their own two-seater runabouts, or stepped from big shiny motor-cars driven by the family chauffeur. The sort of young women who would never have to hang out the washing before putting a small child in the pram with the baby and pushing it for an hour to get to town on market day.

Iris laughed down at her two little ones and jogged the pram.

"But today we're as rich as anyone!" she told them.

She bought yards of flowery cotton for dresses, a length of flannel for trousers, and a twist of toffee for the little girl. Even putting some aside for shoes, there was enough left to buy herself something at Cushings. She knew what she wanted. A small tea service. Just enough for two in the brightest, gayest, pattern in the window.

Iris tucked her prize into the pram like another baby and wheeled it all home.

Tom laughed when she told him some chap had paid her money for the old vases.

"Who was it gave us those, Tom?"

"Them up at the big house, my last job. I can remember it now. Said they was from Worcester and they was a hundred and fifty years old. Like I should be pleased, they said it. With all their money they could have bought us something new for a wedding present. That's your betters for you."

Iris did not mention her mother's locket and rings. They were her things. Tom didn't need to know about them.

"But do you like the tea set, Tom?"

"It's nice and bright. Cheerful-like. Funny name for it, Bizarre."

"Yes," said Iris, gazing fondly on the china items laid out on the table, "I never had cups and saucers with a pattern I knew the name of before. And all matching."

"Shall we have a cup of tea, then?" asked Tom.

"Oh, no. These are for best."

Carefully, Iris packed it all back into its own bright box and put the box on the top shelf of the cupboard where the vases had stood.

When her eldest daughter got engaged, Iris took down the box and looked at the bright china briefly. Somehow it had never looked quite right in the cottage.

"Here, lovey, you have it. It's never been used."

Iris's daughter, who moved with her husband to a small flat in London, never used it either but she got a few bob for it from a man who called at the door.

Christmas Spirit

The night grew colder. The central heating had switched itself off hours ago. Stars were glittering in the black sky like chips of ice.

Michael Tindall stirred in his dreams and pushed himself deeper under the warm duvet. His feet emerged at the bottom and chilled rapidly. His attempts to sort out his bedcovers without quite waking himself up were in vain.

"I don't hold with these doovette things," said a voice in the darkness, "Always had blankets myself. Firmly tucked in."

Michael experienced the unpleasant sensation of his scalp crawling. It was as if it was trying to sneak off with his hair.

He peered over his covers. There was a shape by the window. Michael always opened his curtains before getting into bed because he enjoyed being greeted by the morning light each day. When you are forty-five and live alone you can do what you like with your own curtains.

"Ah, you're awake. I used to go in for rattling chains and whoo-oo noises and so on, but these days I can't be bothered. What happened to next-door?"

Someone was sitting on the chair by the window. Michael could see the icy stars through his visitor.

He wanted to leap out and rush screaming from the room, but his nose told him it was freezing out there. He knew he should demand in the justified manner of the affronted householder what the hell whoever-it-was was doing in his bedroom, but he was too startled to speak. And he was somewhat puzzled by the reference to next door.

One thing he was clear on. He was now wide awake.

His visitor had apparently been passing the time by reading one of Michael's books.

"Old toys, eh? Is that what you're interested in? You a dealer or a collector?"

"Both. What do you mean - what happened to next-door? Who are you anyway?"

"Who *was* I. Past tense, obviously. I suppose you might say I'm a tormented spirit. Well, I used to be tormented, but you can get used to anything. Where's your shop, then? Got any automata? Or toy soldiers? What sort of price do they go for nowadays? I used to have a lovely set of soldiers. There were cavalry, infantry, cannon, whole battalions......"

"Listen," Michael interrupted angrily, "I get enough people coming in and boring on about the toys they had as kids without being woken up in the middle of a freezing cold night ...."

"Right, yes, fair enough. That's not what I'm here for. We'll get on with it then. Of course, I should be next-door. What happened to it?"

"How should I know? It was gone before I arrived. In the war, I should think."

"Which one? Boer or Great?"

"World War II. Where've you been?"

The shape by the window drooped disconsolately.

"I don't get out as much as I used to."

"Oh."

There was a little awkward silence. Then they both tried to speak at once.

"No, no. It's all right. You go ahead," said Michael, graciously.

"It's the manifesting. It takes it out of you. I used to do it all the time at first, then it was down to once a year. But I don't even manage that now. I last gave a good haunting in December 1921. I got a maid into trouble."

Michael blinked.

"She dropped the Rockingham tea-service. There was a terrible fuss about it. Threats of stopped wages, all that sort of thing. I had to nip off through the wall sharpish. I was supposed to be pointing out the error of his ways to the head of the household, not frightening 14 year old girls with trays in their hands."

"Er, when did you, um....?"

"Shrug off this mortal coil? Let's see now. I think it was before Waterloo. No, I tell a lie, I remember hearing about Boney's retreat from Moscow when I was about nine or ten, so it couldn't have been. Mine was a death in maturity. In my prime, actually. I was not ready, I had plans. Oh, yes! Of course, that's when you get the manifesting."

"How did you, um....?"

"Meet my end? Dug my grave with my teeth. I used to be a tremendous trencherman, you'd have been proud of the way I could see off a joint of meat, two puddings, and a good piece of cheese. I still miss Stilton. Anyway, I was taken off with the apoplexy at the dinner table. But I'm digressing. We need to sort you out before I fade."

"Sort *me* out?" asked Michael, "I thought you said you were supposed to be next door?"

"You see, it's a kind of magnetism. If one ..er...*hauntee*, shall we say, isn't where they're supposed to be you get attracted to the next nearest one.

That's you."

Michael swallowed hard. His visitor's joviality had vanished. Those last words rang with real menace. Michael realised he was trembling. He felt horribly hollow.

"Wha........?" The words wouldn't come.

"What have you done to deserve this?" said the shape, rising from the chair and growing higher and darker. "I'll show you, Michael Tindall. Come with me!"

Michael had no sensation of moving, but saw beneath him a sitting room in an old folks' residential home and a person he recognised.

The shadowy shape had somehow encircled him but it's voice seemed to come from some distance away.

"You know her, don't you?"

Michael stared down on the only youthful person in the room. She was Marilyn Smith. Just a week ago she had brought him a rocking horse, two pairs of Victorian ice-skates, a very early teddy-bear and various other things and said there would be much more to come. He watched her bending over an elderly man in elderly tweeds. She tucked a rug over the old man's knees and looked up from his unresponsive figure with a pleased little smile.

"How much do you think she gave him?" asked the distant voice.

"I didn't know!" said Michael, desperately.

"Didn't you?" persisted the voice. "Did you really believe she had a house crammed with collectables? So many interesting old toys to sell you time after time?"

"Well, I knew she worked with old people, she told me that, but I never thought....."

"Onward, Michael Tindall! There's more!"

Below him Michael saw bare floorboards. A middle-aged woman and a very young man watched two removals men manoeuvre a sofa through the front door.

"I don't understand, William," the woman was saying, "There's *nothing* up there? Where's the rocking horse? Where's Grandpa's old bear? There can't be nothing up there!"

"Honestly, Mother, there's nothing at all."

"What can he have done with all those things? He mentioned them specially just last week."

"Mother," said the young man gently, "He was getting very .....forgetful. He probably sold them years ago. Don't cry. Try not to mind."

"What am I supposed to do?" demanded Michael.

The distant voice came closer. It was almost flippant.

"Oh, I'm sure you'll think of something. Let's get back."

Michael looked around. He was hovering just above the neglected grass by his garden fence.

"Why are we here?"

"Oh, this is just a bit of nostalgia for me. See that mound? That used to be our kitchen. And that bit with the nettles was our parlour. I used to play on the floor in front of the fire there. I was quite looking forward to having a look round the old place while I was scaring some sense into the old sinner who lived there. Pity I missed him. Right, that's it. You can find your own way back from here, can't you?"

Michael's bare feet hit the grass and he stumbled onto his knees. The grass crunched and frost melted into his pyjamas.

He heard a chuckle and a cheery voice called, "Soon be Christmas!"

Freezing cold, with damp knees and numb feet, Michael was forced to climb back into his own house through the window of the downstairs loo.

Back in bed with two hot-water bottles and hot chocolate with a nip of brandy, Michael reviewed events.

He had given the foxy-faced Marilyn Smith very fair prices. He had done nothing wrong. His conscience was clear. His conscience had been clear.

Outside cold stars winked in a paling sky. As the sun at the horizon washed a few pleasing pastel colours over it, Michael dozed. When the mug in his hand tilted and the dregs of his chocolate drink sloshed onto his chest, he was jolted awake again.

Crossly, he stripped off his pyjama jacket and went to take a shower.

Being exhausted can be quite galvanising. Focusing only on those things most important to him at this moment, Michael became quite uncharacteristically dynamic.

He was outside the Residential Home as Marilyn Smith came off night-duty. She tried to hurry away, but Michael was determined to be heard.

"All right!" she snapped, "You can have the money back, but I ain't getting involved in nothing else. Here, I'll write their address. You sort it out. I'm off."

"You know," said Michael, "You have a look about you."

"What? What sort of look?"

"Haunted," said Michael and got into his car.

He obtained the telephone number from directory enquiries and made the difficult call. The woman sounded so relieved, so pleased, to be offered her father's things back, Michael was embarrassed.

She wanted to reward him in some way.

"It isn't that they're valuable," she said, "They were Dad's when he was a boy, some were his father's. They're family things."

In the end Michael was persuaded to name something he really wanted. She sent her son, William, to his shop with it.

"I've had a go with one of these," said William, "Dug up a few Roman coins once."

"I'm going to run it over a rough bit of my garden," said Michael, "Please thank your mother. I'm totally overwhelmed."

At three-thirty on Christmas Eve it was growing dark when the metal-detector changed note. Michael switched it off, removed the headset, and marked the spot.

He woke at daybreak on Christmas Day, as excited as if he was a boy again. Thankful he had no near neighbours to think him peculiar, and that the weather was milder, he attacked the ground by the marker.

When his sister called at one o'clock to see why he had not arrived yet for Christmas dinner, he had the Duke of Wellington on horseback in his hand and a grubby lead army all over his kitchen table. He had just spent his happiest Christmas morning. Ever.

The Terracotta Cat

Tariq took down the terracotta cat. It was barely recognizable as a member of the feline species, let alone a representation of the cat goddess herself. The whole thing had a definite wobble. The scratches that were meant to be Bastet's necklace and intricate breast ornament had almost disappeared in the firing.

Tariq's master, a kindly man, seeing the terrible disappointment on the boy's face at the sight of his first apprentice piece, had smiled and told him Bastet's eyes were very fine. Eyes, he said, were notoriously difficult and for Tariq to have made the expression so regal and so enigmatic was a good sign. Tariq would make a fine craftsman. In time. With much practice.

Tariq had carried the piece home and it had been placed on his mother's shelf with the pictures of his father and his three older brothers, all killed in the early days of the War. The village had tried to defend itself against the invading German-Axis forces, but to no avail.

His grandfather, left sightless, sat by the hearth, thinking his inward angry thoughts. Tariq had always been afraid of the fierce old man. He and his mother had not told him Tariq was apprenticed to the local potter for fear of his wrath. Tariq did not offer the terracotta Bastet to him to handle and understand with his chilly knarled fingers.

Made with the unskilled hands of Tariq the apprentice, the terracotta cat seemed so much smaller now in the accomplished hands of Tariq the journeyman.

Three years and much practice had made him a fine craftsman, making all manner of pots and ornamental items which he sold in the bazaar, but although he worked hard and lived frugally, there was just not enough money to fulfil his dreams of freeing his mother from her daily drudgery, cooking on an oil stove in their room above a butcher's shop plagued with flies, carrying water up from the yard shared by so many other families in the quarter, and sewing leather items until her eyes ached and her fingers grew the callouses Tariq had so disliked the touch of when he was a child.

His grandfather was angry until the day he died that Tariq had not followed in the footsteps of himself, his son, and his other grandsons. He said Tariq had not the stomach of a proper man if he could not slaughter, drain, and joint meat. Tariq bore the criticism tranquilly. Since his grandfather could no longer see him to catch hold of him with his huge cold hands, he could no longer beat him.

The German soldier had come to him late, just as Tariq was shutting up his booth for the night. The man had a plan, a simple thing, and would pay Tariq well. Tariq listened attentively, forming plans of his own.

"Mother," he said, sitting down to their evening meal, "Since my grandfather died, I am the head of the household. I need to make better provision for us, I want to move us from this place to somewhere with a cool shaded courtyard all our own, with our own gate. And someone to cook for us. Somewhere I might in time bring a wife who will be a companion to you."

His mother gave a soft laugh.

"You dream, my son. You always did. We might as well imagine leaving this place and going to England, where the British King lives, or to America, where everyone is rich and has refrigerators."

However affectionately meant, her words stung. Their reality pricked Tariq's hide like a barb. But at eighteen he knew he was clever and energetic and his mother was old, nearly forty, and tired by her hard life and her grief.

"I will show you I can provide properly for us!" he said, hotly, "I have an idea that will make us rich!"

Simple ideas are the best ideas. They arrive so clearly that it is always a wonder they have not been thought of before. It was a wonder to Tariq.

He worked the simple idea for the remaining time the Axis forces held sway and his wealth increased swiftly. He bought a nice house with the proceeds. The house had a shady courtyard and a good high gate. He had not only someone to cook for his mother and himself, but someone to clean, and someone to tend the courtyard garden. He found himself a wife who was gentle and a good companion to his mother. When he moved to his nice house, he took with him his apprentice piece. The wobbly terracotta cat had been very good to him. Her likeness, many times repeated, had made his fortune.

He had reasoned that if one common soldier considered it worthwhile to smuggle a small artefact from the tomb of a pharaoh inside a clay ornament home to Germany, then it might just be worthwhile to repeat the exercise.

After the soldier, four of his comrades came to his booth with little looted items they had rescued before they were loaded onto the Nazi treasure trains and Tariq dressed them in a coat of clay, a rather finer copy of his early cat but still a little wobbly, a cheap souvenir, something no-one would look at twice. When the last one came, Tariq made for him a very fine model of Bastet indeed, as fine as any that might have been stolen from a pharaoh's tomb.

It was brought back to him by an officer who believed it had been and confiscated it, but came to check where the soldier had desperately told him he got it. This was what Tariq had been hoping for. He broke the cat before the officer's astonished eyes to reveal the pilfered artefact within.

The officer stared at the shards for a long while, and Tariq explained what he had been doing. He showed the officer some examples of his work.

"I don't fire these, of course, because of what goes in them. I dry them in the cooling kiln. This here I've given a special coating of my own devising to look like base metal. In the base of some I put a stone that is quite visible, to account for the weight. They are coarse and cheap in appearance and so do not attract any attention. These on display, are what I usually make to sell. They are rather better, as you see."

"My friend," said the officer, smiling, "I think we can come to a very satisfactory arrangement together. But you are now off-limits to my men, you understand?"

One day in 1943, a British officer came to Tariq's booth where Tariq's assistant attended on him. The officer selected some pots and chose a foot-high model of Bastet from the back of the booth that was not of first quality. The assistant accepted payment and turned to bring wrapping to the board counter. Turning back he was in time to witness the British officer smashing the items one after another on the ground. Shaking his head at the lunacy of the Englishman, he watched the officer crouch down and sort through the smashed pieces. After a few minutes the man straightened up.

"Don't bother to wrap them," he said and turning smartly walked away.

The assistant came out from the booth to stare after him and saw him repeat the same action at another pottery booth. And another. After buying and smashing items at each pottery booth in sight the British officer went away.

The pottery sellers in striped djellabas fluttered out into the dusty alley of the bazaar, bowing their heads together, and animatedly discussed this strange behaviour. They waved and pointed in amazement at the smashed and ruined pots and ornaments. When they had given the incident a satisfactorily thorough airing, and had apprentices sweep up the shards, they went back shrugging to their booths to continue with business.

At the end of the day Tariq's assistant locked up the booth and carried the takings to Tariq's house. He told Tariq about the British officer.

Tariq laughed, clapped the man on the shoulder and told him the English went mad in the heat, everyone knew that.

When his assistant had gone, Tariq sighed and grew sad. He had his nice house and his life had become very comfortable, but as soon as the British had come his brief but very lucrative business with Germany was really over. There was a continuing trickle of visitors to his booth with special requirements, but soon even those grown wealthy from their wartime plunder would be unable to hide from their avengers, their minions would be caught, and their addiction to pillaged treasures would be brought forcibly to an end. The British were all over the place. Now Tariq knew the British knew all about his speciality, except who he was. It was so very vexing.

Tariq went inside and stood gazing at Bastet's wobbly representation until his mother came in and interrupted his thoughts.

"What are you doing, my son? Are you coming to eat with us? Why are you so sad and silent?"

"Just dreaming, mother, of what might of been."

His mother looked pleased.

"Oh, yes. We might have been still living over that terrible butcher's shop without your dreams."

As he followed her to the table where his wife waited for him with steaming plates of good food, he carried his apprentice piece with him.
His mind was already working on the situation.

If only he had been at his booth himself today when the British officer came he might have had some lucrative business with him instead.

"I think you will have to put the little cat down while you eat, Tariq!" His wife laughed across the low table at him.

Tariq put the misshaped terracotta cat down on the table in front of him. He stared at it while he ate.

There was always tomorrow.

The British might be here for some time.

Sporting Chance

A thin child in plaits, wearing a cotton dress made from a pattern that promised a little girl's summer frock from half a yard of material, ran up to the improvised net that stretched over the last un-dug bit of lawn and successfully whacked the ball back over it. The boy on the other side, somewhat older, back-handed the ball out into the vegetables, narrowly missing a man in braces beside a wheelbarrow. The man straightened up with the ball in his hand. Scowling, he hurled it back to the children.

"Time you packed that in," he said to the girl, "Missus'll want the hens shut up for the night. You," he addressed the boy, "wheel this to the muck-heap. There's a war on, you know!" He snorted. "I wouldn't have you lot round my feet, else. Reserved occupation, me," he added proudly and after a moment's slow thought, asked, "Where'd you get those bats, anyroad?"

"In the 'ouse," said the boy truculently. He was a Londoner like the girl but from a poorer part, "Missus said we could use 'em."

"They're only old ones no-one wants," said the girl.

"You better be truthing," said the man, maliciously, "I'll be asking Missus!"

"Sophie! Come on! We're going now!"

A small figure in a full white dress with a blue sash and bow and an oversize straw hat, whipped her hands hastily behind her back and turned to look innocently towards her parents on the terrace. She had been about to pick the biggest red bloom on the peony bush at the end of the overgrown lawn.

Not fooled for a moment, but enchanted by the image, Tom Walker said, "When we were getting into the car at home that party dress looked so ridiculous......."

"Easier to let her wear it, though, than have a tantrum for all the neighbours to see," commented his wife, shifting the baby to her other hip, "And that's *my* hat she's got on."

"She looks so sweet here - a sentimental portrait of an idyllic Victorian childhood."

Sophie, hand on hat, ran up the lawn, shiny red shoes and frilly socks twinkling, white dress fluttering. Tom held out his arms and swung her up, losing the hat in the process.

"You look gorgeous," he said, "Even though we know you're really quite horrid."

Sophie laughed.

"What's gorjus?"

Sophie's mother said, "You might rescue my hat from the flowerbed."

In the car, they pointed out the problems to each other.

"The garden would be hard work."

"The roof needs attention."

"Dreadful kitchen."

"The decor!"

"Have to have a proper survey."

"More expense."

There was a silence.

"The barn seemed sound."

"French doors on to the terrace."

"Stained glass panels by the front door."

"Reflected a nice pattern on the wall when the sun shone."

"Did you like it, Sophie?"

Sophie in the back, busy caring for her electronic virtual pet, said, "My room was nice."

"Oh? Which was your room?"

"The one with the picture of the lady in a long dress. She can watch me when I'm asleep."

"Good grief!" exclaimed her father softly, "Where does she get her ideas?"

"Not my side of the family," said her mother, firmly, "we're practical. It's your side that's arty-farty."

Hearing this, Sophie shouted with laughter.

"That's enough, Sophie!" snapped her mother.

"We'll make an offer then, Sara?" Tom said.

"The executors want a quick sale and they didn't mention the roof - we'll try a few thousand off the price," said Sara.

In the back, the baby chuckled. Sara turned. Sophie was very, very, softly singing to herself. When Sara listened, she found the song had only two words.

On the telephone to her mother-in-law, Sara said, "It's a big step up from our old tall terrace to this place, but hopefully we can make it support us a bit. Tom will tart up the barn for his pictures and antiques, and rent some space to a few other people, and I'm going to do a bit of B &B as well as my upholstery."

"It's a lovely part of the country. I was evacuated out that way during the war with some other children. I was not much older than Sophie. I used to tell the boys about it. I remember once...............,"

"So, we'll see you on Sunday, Marjorie?" Sara cut in mercilessly before

Marjorie could get into her stride. "We should know if our offer's been accepted by then. I think we have a sporting chance."

"Yes, dear," said Marjorie. She did understand how busy Sara was. She and Tom worked so hard. Tom was the youngest - five years younger than Peter, seven years younger than John. Strange to think of Tom buying a great big house. Me and Jack, she thought, were only just thinking of buying our council house at Tom's age. Haven't we all come up in the world? There's Peter doing so well in his company, and John practically famous.

"Bye, Marjorie." Sara hung up.

The cork popped softly from the bottle and six glasses were thrust forward to be filled. Tom grinned as he poured frothing wine into Sara's first.

"Here's to the Mucks in their manor!" toasted John, "You're bloody mad, boy."

"I hope you've thought carefully about the finances, Tom," said Peter, "If you need any advice........."

"Thanks. I know where you live. Bubbly, Mum?"

"Can I have some?" asked Sophie, androgynous today in t-shirt and shorts for an informal family Sunday lunch.

"Nana will find you some lemonade in the kitchen," said Marjorie.

"I'll sort her out," said John's wife - his second, much younger, wife, "C'mon, brat. Let your Nan sit down for five minutes."

Peter's wife, Avril, looking pained, genteelly remonstrated, "You shouldn't call her that, Kerry. Little children's egos are very fragile."

"Spockian cobblers," said Kerry cheerfully and ushered Sophie from the room.

Only two days in residence at their new house and still feeling they were merely camping out among the boxes of their possessions, but not averse to showing the place off, Tom, Sara, Sophie, and baby Jack, dressed in old clothes for the big clean-up, stood on their fine front steps and welcomed the inevitable invasion.

"Let me at a camera!" cried John, leaping out and opening the boot of his sports car.

Peter and Avril assisted Marjorie from the back seat of their Audi saloon.

Sweeping through the house, commenting freely as only family can, they finally poured out onto the terrace to look over the garden.

"Look at Avril," said Kerry softly to John, "Like she's smelt something bad."

"Envy," said John, camera in hand, as the others moved down the weed-filled lawn, "It's her hobby. And Being Right."

"Poor Peter."

"Nah! She cooks like a dream and thinks he's God. She's the perfect wife. Whereas you're useless in the kitchen and you delight in pointing out my short-comings. Dunno what came over me, marrying you."

"Bet you do," said Kerry, unperturbed.

"Yeah, well." John turned slowly, shutter rapidly opening and closing, motor chattering the film on. He called out, "Great place, Tom. Can I use it?"

"I'm not having the place filled with a lot of preening anorexics!" called back Sara.

"Not even for money, Saz? Where's this barn? Can I exhibit some of my stuff there, Tom?"

"Why not? Your name might give us some additional cred."

"What are big brothers for?" said John, pleased.

"Where's Mother?" asked Peter.

"Letting Sophie show her round."

"They're just coming," said Avril, "Marjorie! We're going to see the barn where Tom will have his little Antiques Centre. What's that you've got, Sophie?"

"Art and Antiques Emporium," Tom corrected her.

"Photography, Art and Antiques Store," said John, "Don't be so posh."

"It's hardly changed at all," said Marjorie.

"What's hardly changed, Mum?" asked John.

Tom was staring at Sophie. "Are they what I think they are? Sophie, show Daddy what you've got there."

"They're called rackets. Nana and me are going to play with them. Nana had them when she was a little girl." Sophie broke off, looking puzzled. "In our new house," she added, frowning.

Tom wasn't listening. He took one of the rackets from her arms.

"Peculiar shape," remarked Peter, "The strings are a mess."

"They're all bent," said Avril, "What a shame. They should have been kept in racket presses. Never mind, Sophie dear, Auntie Avril and Uncle Peter will buy you a nice new racket for your birthday. Would you like that?"

"I like this one," said Sophie, twisting away from consolation with the second racket tight to her chest.

"Mum?" Tom suddenly asked, "Was this where you and the other kids.............?"

"That's right, dear," said Marjorie.

"I can't believe it! Why didn't you say?"exclaimed Tom.

"I only saw it today."

"You were evacuated *here* during the war?" asked Peter.

"Amazing," said John. They had heard her stories so often, they were part of their fabric.

"We rigged up some old sacking as a net just here. The gardener wasn't very nice to us, but he wasn't very bright so we didn't take much notice. The Missus was a nice lady, though."

"Dear God," murmured Sara to Kerry, "We've only gone and bought her War-time Reminisces!"

Tom reached for the second racket to look it over. Sophie yelled in protest.

"Oh, let her have them," said Marjorie, "They're just old things. They were old when we used to play with them."

"They're not just old, Mum, they're 19th century. She can't play with them. No, Sophie, listen, they're worth a lot of money .... Look, come inside and we'll find Daddy's racket for you." Tom began to lead his daughter towards the house, the tilted-head tennis rackets under his arm.

"Tom, dear," Marjorie called after them, "There are some other things."

Tom stopped dead and looked back.

"Other things?" said Tom.

Marjorie shrugged.

"There's the croquet sets," she suggested, "Sophie's too little for the cricket bats and old golf clubs and fishing stuff, and the archery things aren't at all suitable. It's all been there years."

"Mum," said Tom, "Where is all this?"

"Through the back of the cleaning cupboard in the kitchen, a sort of storeroom. There used to be another door into it from the back porch, but it's boarded up on that side now."

"Show me," said Tom, coming back and taking her arm firmly.

"Show all of us," said Sara.

Standing aside from the crush and squirm of observers in the cleaning cupboard, listening to the exclamations further in, Marjorie smiled.

"I'll make some tea while you look," she said.

No one responded. Contentedly, she filled the kettle.

The Lucky Teapot

At 8 o'clock on a dark and wet November morning in the year 2001, Emma Scott and her sister Isobel opened the rear of their over-packed 15yr-old Peugeot 205 hatchback outside the venue for a small monthly Antiques Fair where they regularly took a stand and failed between them to prevent a small but determined box of china from tilting and emptying its contents into the road at their feet.

While Isobel threw herself with outstretched arms across the open hatchback to stem the slide of the rest of their stock, Emma with a sorrowful groan knelt on soaking knees and gathered the items on the road back into their box, feeling some of them crunch inside their bubble-wrap in a very un-reassuring manner.

"How bad is it?" asked Isobel, sounding rather strained as she was using her stomach muscles to shove the lowest box back under the next layer, her arm muscles being for the moment unavailable as they were fully employed preventing the escape of two framed 1920's watercolours, a small rug, and some 19th century fire-irons, "Look, you'll have to help here, I daren't move."

"Looks expensive," said Emma, getting up and lifting out the most unstable items from the car, "Okay, you can move now."

They shifted the remainder of the precarious load between them, stacked it on their folding trolley, and wheeled it from the cold dark drizzle into the light and relative warmth of the venue.

"Oh God," said Isobel, unpacking the box of china and exclaiming over each bubble-wrapped parcel, "Oh no. Oh, what a shame. Oh, I really liked that bowl. Oh dear. Oh dear, oh dear. Oh! It's .... yes, it's all right. There you are, Emma, at least the teapot's okay."

Emma took the little rotund teapot with its simple floral decoration from her sister. She examined the spout and checked the handle, carefully put on its lid, and let out a relieved sigh.

"It's 200 years old," she said as she placed it on the display shelves, "It would be such a shame if it got damaged now."

On a very sunny afternoon in July, 1799, two ladies in sprigged muslin gowns crossed a dusty road in Bristol to take tea with their neighbour,

Mrs. Orchard. They folded their parasols on her doorstep and were shown upstairs into an elegant sitting-room.

While the ladies exchanged gossip and the little kettle on the table came up to the boil, Mrs. Orchard unlocked the tea-caddy and mixed her teas for her favourite blend.

One of her chattering visitors, who had been sitting with her hand on her folded parasol now sought to dispose of it somewhere so that her hands would be free to take her cup when it came. She propped it inattentively against a nearby little side-table but from the corner of her eye saw it begin to roll away. Reaching out hastily to grab it before it fell, the lady knocked the little side-table into the table where Mrs. Orchard was preparing tea. The tea-table rocked, the spirit kettle swung in its cradle, and the tea-cups jangled on their saucers.

With an exclaimed apology the lady who was the cause of this leapt up with some idea of preventing further damage and with her un-regarded parasol knocked Mrs. Orchard's brand-new teapot, into which she was just spooning the blended tea, clean off the table.

The ladies watched in horror as the pretty new teapot with its delicate floral decoration on its round body sailed across the elegant room towards the very solid panelled door. Just a moment before the inevitable smash was expected the door was opened by Mrs. Orchard's maid bringing in cake. The teapot bounced off her broad bosom, producing a startled squeak from the poor woman, and veered off, scattering tea leaves as it spun, hurtling straight towards the sofa where Pepe, Mrs. Orchard's little lap-dog lay sleeping. It struck little Pepe a blow on his rump that startled him awake and had him dashing for safety behind the curtains.

The teapot ran out of momentum, rocked a fraction, and settled in the warm hollow of the silk cushion just vacated by the little dog.

Three of the four women let out a collective breath. The fourth fled in shame.

With admirable aplomb, Mrs. Orchard had the tea-leaves swept up, her little dog retrieved trembling from his hiding place and the fortunate teapot replaced on the table, where, mixing a fresh blend of tea as the kettle merrily boiled, she resumed her interrupted conversation with her remaining guest.

On a mild September afternoon in 1812, a young man up at university lost the teapot overboard from the punt where he was entertaining two young ladies. It was fished out safely and returned to him by two young men on another punt happy for the opportunity to gain acquaintance with the young ladies.

In May, on a fresh bright day in 1850, the teapot was knocked off the top of a coach by a careless elbow at Epsom Racecourse where a party of race-goers were picnicking while watching the races. It was caught by a passer-by with excellent reflexes, who was very glad the tea that poured down his suit was nearly cold. The lid fell harmlessly onto the grass.

During the Blitz in the Second World War the teapot was found still intact on a badly damaged London side-board alone in the midst of the shattered shards of a small collection of china shepherdesses, a glass posy vase, and a pair of plaster spaniels. It was one of only two items in the bombed house to survive unharmed. The bed from the first-floor front bedroom was the other and that was found in the next street.

In January, 1965, it snowed and in Oxford, Emma Scott was born. In August of the same year, Emma's grandmother died. All her grandmother's possessions were packed up with the intention of sending them to auction, but Emma's charming, but vague, academic parents never got round to it.

In March, 1970, as the wind roared round the house, Isobel Scott was born and was heartily resented by five-year-old Emma. However, by the following year Emma decided she quite liked her.

In October, 2001, their father retired and while helping their parents pack for a move from the large rambling house in the centre of Oxford to a smaller, more manageable, house on the outskirts, Emma and Isobel found their late grandmother's belongings at the back of the loft.

"Oh, yes," said their mother, putting on her half-glasses and peering at the faded identifying labels, "I seem to remember she had some quite nice things. She loved poking about in antique shops. No good to us, though. What do you think? Do you think people might want this old stuff?"

Emma, who bought things at auction and with her sister Isobel's help, sold them at small Antiques Fairs, thought they might.

"Well, you take them and see how you do, dears."

Emma looked over a round-bodied teapot simply decorated with a delicate floral design. Her researches confirmed to her that it was late 18th century, hard-paste porcelain, almost certainly from Bristol or Plymouth. It was in perfect condition.

"Probably kept in a cabinet and never used," she remarked to Isobel.

At 5 o'clock on a day in November 2001 that was still just as wet as when it begun, after a pretty good but not exceptional day, Emma and Isobel were packing.

While the venue's caretaker crashed and stacked tables around them with excessive noise and vigour, someone opened a concealed door hitting the end of the folding display stand where the 18th century teapot, which they had not sold, stood waiting to be packed.

The display stand swayed. The caretaker's assistant peeked round the door to see what was resisting his opening it fully.

"Oh, no!" cried Emma and Isobel together.

The lid came off and rolled on the table as the teapot left visible support and headed left, missing the edge of the table and disappearing below.

It bounced once on Isobel's folded raincoat on the floor and rolled off on to a dropped table cover belonging to the next stand.

The lady on the next stand didn't see it and was just reaching down to pick up her table cover to fold it. Emma pounced and snatched the teapot up in both shaking hands. Isobel grabbed the lid.

When their car was loaded, Isobel drove while Emma cradled the teapot, cosseted in extra bubble-wrap, on her lap.

"We're not going to sell it, are we?" asked Isobel.

"No," agreed Emma. "It's probably had more close calls today than in all its life. It's one lucky teapot. We won't tempt fate any further."

Future Tense

It had a segmented dial in bright colours, like multi-coloured slices of pie, and a pointer that spun round the dial and stopped on a red or yellow or blue or green or plain white slice. Across the top was written:

Will You Ever Be Worth A Fortune?
Are You Worth Your Weight in Gold?
Step on the platform and find out!
6d.

With each slice having a value from the vague but very desirable: *Your Weight in Gold*, through nice solid sums ranging from *£100* to *£1,000,000*, and including, on the plain white, the utterly disillusioning: *One Week's Wages*, this was a Fortune-telling machine in the most literal sense. It claimed to tell you the most you would ever be worth.

At the age of fifteen, with school days drawing to a close, the idea of possessing that knowledge was irresistible. After a hurried sorting out of sixpences amongst themselves, one by one the girls stepped on the platform.

Sonia's was a very satisfactory amount in the thousands. It seemed vast riches to someone who rarely ever mentioned proposed school outings at home because she knew there was no money to pay for them. As this outing to an area of outstanding natural beauty was regarded as educational and the coach was being paid for by the local authority, today's trip only required a packed lunch and so Sonia was able to be here.

Hazel, the drama queen, made a big show of being scared of what the machine might tell her, forcing the other two to push her, squealing, onto the platform and put her sixpence in the slot for her. Then she couldn't look, didn't dare. She needn't have made all that fuss, she was going to be a millionaire. Kay secretly thought Hazel would most likely marry one rather than become one by the sweat of her own exquisite brow.

Kay stepped up to discover the full extent of her future monetary value, inserted her sixpence, and watched the pointer spin, slow, waver and stop.

Her shoulders drooped. She was close to tears. The plain white slice was her fortune. One weeks' wages.

What a hand-to-mouth fate loomed before her. Scraping by, making do, never desiring nice things because they would never be within her reach. Living a poor desperate life in fear of the knock of rent collector, like Sonia's parents. Kay wanted Hazel's life, one of ease and comfort, with kind well-off parents who bought their only child anything she wanted.

Seeing the Fortune Machine's prediction for Kay, the other two tried frantically to console her. Generous Hazel, who liked happy people around her, insisted Kay have another go, pressing a sixpence into her hand.

Grudgingly, this time the machine awarded Kay £100. But she didn't really believe it. And compared to Sonia's thousands and Hazel's million, it was a pittance. It was her value. The most she would ever be worth. And anyway, everyone knew it was the first answer that counted. Kay was miserable.

Hazel did her best, hugging Kay, clowning for her, and to please Hazel for all this effort Kay shrugged it off. She put on the smile her friends wanted to see and they made their way back to the waiting coach.

As the driver swung the coach onto the main road, the three knelt up on the rear seat to look back at the receding beauty spot, until strict Miss Ellis saw them, reminded them they were young ladies not urchins, and made them sit properly.

"It was a strange place, though," said Sonia, "to put a fortune machine."

"Middle of nowhere, really," said Hazel, "Just in a not very nice toilet, without even any hot water. Isn't it funny how there are always two taps and both of them for cold water – why do they do it? They could have just one and not raise our expectations."

"What would a good week's wages be?" asked Kay. She and Sonia waited for Hazel to answer, they had no idea what people earned. Such things were not talked about in their houses.

"Well, since we're Grammar School girls we might get seven pounds a week when we leave and get nice jobs in a bank or an office."

"Does us being at Grammar School make some sort of difference?" asked Kay.

Hazel rolled her eyes.

"You two are so naïve. You don't know anything. How did you get to Grammar school?"

"Passed the eleven-plus," said Sonia.

"And passed the interview with the headmistress," said Kay.

"Didn't anyone tell you what a good opportunity it was for you?" prompted Hazel, "How lucky you were?

"Well, yes, but my dad never stopped complaining about buying the uniform – as if it was a surprise for him and some sort of punishment for me being clever or something," said Kay, remembering her father shouting he wasn't having it. She could go to the secondary modern like her brothers. He wasn't paying some posh outfitters for stuff you could get on the market at half the price.

"You could have got second-hand like I did," said Sonia. But Kay knew that second-hand clothes wouldn't be allowed in her house. Better not to go to this school at all if his daughter had to wear second-hand clothes, was her father's view. In the end her uncle and aunt offered to pay for her uniform. Her father's pride wouldn't let him accept, of course. Somehow the uniform was bought. Her mother never stopped reminding Kay how good her father was to her and how grateful she should be.

Kay asked her parents hardly more often than Sonia for money for outings. Certainly she knew neither of them would be going on the ski-ing trip next year.

On seven pounds a week there didn't seem much likelihood of going ski-ing ever.

When the time came, Kay left school. University was out of the question. She couldn't expect her parents to keep her for another four or five years. She was lucky they let her stay on past the age of fifteen. She should be grateful. She had six O-levels and low expectations.

Kay got a nice job in an office. Kay got some promotion. Kay married and had a daughter. Kay stayed with the same company for many years. Kay was made redundant. Kay reviewed her situation and came to a decision.

Kay swished, zigzagging down the slope, and came to a dramatic halt in a spray of white powdery snow. She laughed.

Kay went home to change her life.

Eight years later she stood before the same Fortune Machine. It might be one just like it, but somehow Kay thought there had only ever been this one. She had never really expected to see it again.

"Well, Mum, are you going to get on it?"

"Yes, in a moment. I just want to think about Sonia and Hazel for a moment. Sonia left school at the same time as me. She got seven O-levels – she took Religious Studies as an extra. And she got married within the year. Hazel stayed on and went into the Sixth-form and then on to drama school. She did a bit of telly, had a small role in a West End play, and then left grey drizzly England for sunny America. Sonia won the football pools and moved to Spain with her husband and two sons. Hazel lives in California and keeps a flat in London."

"She married a millionaire?"

"Not exactly. She married another struggling actor. They both worked very hard and they both got lucky in films. They might well be millionaires now."

"Go on, here's an old sixpence, I want to see what it says about you now."

Kay stepped onto the platform, her daughter, Hannah, put the old sixpence in the slot.

Nothing happened. Kay burst out laughing.

"The pointer is jammed," she said.

"Oh," said Hannah, disappointed, "I wanted to do mine as well."

"They often rust up. People leave them in damp sheds. Forgotten for years. It doesn't matter. It's the first answer that counts and we know what that was."

"Yes, *One Week's Wages*. I know."

"You know what I earned last week?"

"Of course I do, I *am* the firm's accountant."

"And was it lots?"

Hannah grinned.

"It was lots and lots - our best week ever."

"That's all right then," said Kay.

She put an arm about Hannah and walked with her past row upon row of early amusement machines. There were one-armed bandits, what-the-butler-saw, test your strength, and, the firm's speciality, fortune-telling machines of every imaginable kind. Two men were overhauling one of the machines. Kay paused beside them.

"Could you have a look at that what-you're-worth machine we just got in?" she said, "Hannah wants to know how rich she's going to be."

"Right you are, we'll do it next," said one of the men. "This one's all ready for shipping." He put a coin in the machine's slot and it sprouted a ticket. "Here you are, Kay, have this one on me."

Kay pulled the rectangle of pasteboard from the slot.

"*You are going on a journey,*" she read aloud. She turned to Hannah. "That'll be ski-ing again this weekend, then."

"Great, Mum," said Hannah.

"How the bosses live, eh?" said one man amiably to the other as they moved off down the warehouse to work on Kay's latest acquisition.

The Killing

"Going like hot cakes," boasted Ian Green. He patted the late Victorian bedside commode he had just unloaded from his vehicle with the help of Craig, a sort of nephew-by-marriage. "Can't get enough of them. I've got this bloke who comes to every fair. He's had three off me already. "

Ian Green turned away from Craig to see what his other helper was up to.

"Haven't you got stalled out yet?" he said irritably to the little mouse of a woman who was on her knees, unpacking smalls from a Ffyes banana box.

"Sorry, Ian, me back's playing up. You couldn't lift this box onto the table for me, could you?"

Ian Green gave Craig an eyes to heaven look and a nod over his shoulder. Craig went to lift the box.

Craig was a good boy, thought Ian, very willing, and costing him almost nothing. His mum talked about college, but Craig was getting the chance here to learn all he needed to know from a real pro.

"Right, Craig, let's shift the last few bits off the wagon."

"Why does this bloke want so many Victorian commodes?" asked Craig as they lifted out a table.

"He's a collector," answered Ian Green, who had never enquired,

"Anyway no one else seems to want them, so I just count myself lucky finding him. Marnie! Get some tea made."

"I'll do it," offered Craig.

Ian Green shook his head.

"No. You and me do the heavy work. Marnie does the smalls and the tea - and as she's told." He gave a laugh at his own witticism.

Craig frowned.

An early trade buyer was looking over a pine bookcase, and Craig stood by watching while his sort-of uncle made the first sale of the day. Craig was unsure about their exact relationship, but since he was definitely not a blood relation, Craig couldn't bring himself to call him Uncle Ian, so he jocularly shortened it to Unk.

The bookcase sold and the tea drunk, Unk said, "We'll see if there's anything about worth buying. Watch and learn, son."

Looking round, with Ian Green airing his knowledge without restraint, Craig perceived more than a few sardonic glances their way.

Spotting another commode, this one in mahogany, he eagerly pointed it out only to have his extended arm hastily slapped down and Unk fiercely hissing under his breath, "Don't pounce on the bloody thing!"

But the stall-holder was sharply alert to any show of interest.

"Dead cheap," he said, "£50 trade."

Ian Green pursed his lips. It was very cheap, and quite an early one, but he had a lad to educate.

"I can't go more than £45," he said, "and that's more than I usually pay for these."

The stall-holder sighed. "Go on, then. A fiver's nothing one way or the other to me. If it matters that much to you, have it for £45."

Craig suppressed a grin at the put-down, but Unk seemed unaware of it as he peeled notes from a thick wad.

"I can't normally shift these," admitted the stall-holder, pocketing the money, "You find they sell, do you?"

"No problem," bragged Ian Green, "Got a regular buyer. Take this back for us, Craig. I'll see you a bit later."

Craig hefted their purchase and carried it back to their stall.

Marnie eyed the item with some doubt.

"Another one?"

Craig shrugged.

"I'd better just phone the man up." Marnie fished a mobile phone from her shoulder bag and keyed in numbers from a battered address book. After a minute or so, she disconnected. "No answer. He'll be on his way."

Craig thought she looked very unwell. Tiny in stature and with fine light hair straggling unevenly beneath a knitted hat, she had parchment thin skin over sharp cheekbones and purple beneath her eyes. From time to time she put a hand to the small of her back, lifting her shoulders to ease an obvious discomfort.

"You should get Unk to rub your back for you," Craig said, with a grin.

Marnie shot him a look that gave this possibility similar odds to a lottery win.

"Why don't you sit down for a bit?" suggested Craig.

"Ian wouldn't like it. He says you can't sell sitting down."

Craig couldn't help himself. He had to ask the intrusive question.

"Why do you put up with him?"

Marnie didn't answer immediately. She looked at Craig warily. After a few moments she said, "Don't worry about me."

It was an order.

"Here he comes," said Craig, warningly to Marnie a little later.

Marnie fumbled the mobile phone from her bag.

"I've tried ringing him," she blurted anxiously, as soon as Ian Green reached her, "But there's no reply."

He ignored her.

Marnie hovered with the mobile in her hand. "I'll try him again."

"Just get me something to eat."

Marnie had the phone to her ear.

"Marnie! I said, get me something to eat!"

Marnie did a little dance, flapping one hand to indicate her call had connected, and trying to come back to Ian at the same time as go and fetch their sandwiches. Her feet decided on the sandwiches, and with the phone in her hand she disappeared behind the vehicle.

She returned with the mobile back in her bag and the sandwiches in her hand.

"What have you sold?" demanded Ian Green, stuffing a ham sandwich into his red face.

Marnie recited her sales. Ian Green looked at his watch and gazed over the dribble of buyers who drifted in and out of the marquees and peered at goods on tables under awnings. The day had started grey and chilly, but now the sun came out fully and people began to unbutton and discard outer garments. Finally, they were down to shirtsleeves and in some cases, grubby vests. Marnie took off her knitted hat and shoved ineffectually at her flattened hair.

"You're looking peaky," remarked Ian Green, "You should sort yourself out."

Craig felt himself boiling, and it wasn't just the heat of the sun.

"All right if I walk round a bit?" he asked.

"All right. Don't be long and don't buy anything."

Craig was back in under half an hour. He was accompanied by two men, each carrying a commode, one in walnut and one with chinoiserie decoration. Craig himself carried one in a distinctly Arts and Crafts style.

"What's this?" asked Ian Green, angrily, "Bloody home delivery?"

"Just for you to see, Unk, no obligation," said Craig.

"Really good price, if you're interested," said one of the men.

Eventually a deal was struck and the men left. Unk turned on Craig.

"Don't you *ever* do anything like that again!"

"No, Unk. Sorry."

A stout man in a string vest strolled up interrupting the reprimand.

"You Ian Green?" he asked. Ian Green said he was. "Heard you wanted Vicky commodes. I've got three or four nice ones on the wagon. Hundred and fifty. Take it or leave it."

"Well, is it three or is it four?"

"Could be five - do you want a look?"

Craig went too, feeling a mad little frisson of glee. It was six. Money was argued about. Money changed hands. They carried the commodes back and put them with the rest. Barely had they set them down when another man came to offer Ian Green two more. Then another with another one.

Ian Green put away his thin wad of notes.

He confidently surveyed his haul. He saw his customer emerge from the throng and approach. He was going to make a killing.

"Mr. Green," the man greeted him, genially, "I believe you have another commode for me. Excellent, excellent."

"I've got a real treat for you this time," declared Ian Green.

"And is this your son?" the customer asked him, smiling on Craig.

"No. He's family, but I don't have any kids. Never wanted 'em."

"Good," said the customer in his genial way. Craig thought it an odd response.

"Marnie!" called Ian Green, over his shoulder, "Marnie'll get you some tea, and you can look over the commodes."

"Commodes," echoed the man, as Marnie hurried to find a cup, "Quite a selection, I shall have a hard time choosing."

Craig saw parts of Unk's face fade from deep red to light purple. A most unhealthy colour.

"Choosing?"

"Umm," murmured the customer, wandering dreamily among the commodes, touching this one and that, opening and closing doors.

Craig, standing behind Unk, bit his lip to suppress a silly giggle that was threatening to disgrace him. Marnie smiled up at the customer as she handed him his tea. Craig had never seen her smile. There was a terrible expectancy in the air. Several nearby stall-holders seemed to sense it too, and aligned themselves like radio telescopes ready to receive whatever was coming.

"A magnificent collection. Does you proud," said the customer, "I should like to take them all."

Ian Green let out the breath he did not realise he had been holding. His colour revived. He prepared to discuss money.

The customer held up a warning hand. He hadn't finished.

"I should *like* to," he said, "But I only need one. The black chinoiserie design, perhaps? Then again, there's the Arts and Crafts one. I think I'll let my sister decide. As a parting gesture. Marnie?"

"The Arts and Crafts one," said Marnie, promptly, "Definitely. Offer him ninety-five, not a penny more."

"His sister? *You?* Pah! Him all posh and you common as muck? Don't make me laugh!"

"Same father," said the customer, calmly, "Different blankets. The old man popped off and left behind more of a confession than a will. I've been granted a little sister when I thought I was an only child. Now, here's ninety-five pounds. Suppose I give this to you and take the commode and Marnie away with me? Do you have everything you need, Marnie?"

The radio telescopes were receiving all this loud and clear, you could see it on their faces. This was nearly as good as a multiple sale on a quiet day.

The disgracing giggle escaped Craig. Ian Green roared. Marnie picked up a small holdall. Her half-brother stooped to the commode.

"No, let me," said Craig, ducking past his flushed and shouting almost-uncle.

He lifted the commode.

"Well if you're sure," demurred the customer.

"It's my pleasure," Craig assured him.

Ian Green told the three of them graphically just what they could do with themselves and the commode.

"He's got thirteen of those things he won't be able to sell on," commented Marnie as they made their way past entertained on-lookers.

"Yep!" agreed Craig, "Highly suitable item for him to be stuck with."

"I wish I'd thought of it," said Marnie, "I'd have left him with hundreds of them. Thank god he never married me."

"Where are you going?" Craig asked.

"To keep house for Blake," said Marnie, "It's indoor work with no heavy lifting and I'm so happy, I could cry."

"We met in the solicitor's office," said Blake, "Through the old man's will. We had a long talk."

"But why buy the commodes? What are they for, Blake?" asked Craig.

"Two reasons: It was an easy way to see Ian Green for myself, and my cats like them. They sleep in them - with the doors open, naturally - so I got them one each."

Marnie made a sound Craig hadn't heard her make before. She laughed. She took her half-brother's arm.

"He's very, very kind," she said to Craig, "but he needs looking after."

"Can we give you a lift anywhere?" asked Blake.

"Yes, please. I want to get home. I've got college applications to fill in."

* * * * * * * * * *

If you have enjoyed this book, why not order a copy for a friend and brighten up their day?

Copies may be ordered direct from:

Precious Chick Publishing
P.O. Box 56
Wellingborough NN8 1SF

www.preciouschickpublishing.com
Email: gillian.mcnern@ntlworld.com

or

From the bookseller whose details appear below: